Salt Water Town

Tales from Castine, Maine

Photo courtesy of Wilson Museum

By Donald A. Small

Third Printing

Front cover image © by John Gardner, Castine, Maine.

Back cover image, "February Street" by Richard Danforth, 1952.

Used with permission of Wilson Museum, Castine, Maine.

ISBN: 978-0-941238-23-6

LCCN: 2016955255

For Penobscot Books:

Caroline Spear, Editor

Jean Lamontanaro, Cover Design, Book Design, Layout

Published by

Penobscot Books

a division of Penobscot Bay Press Community Information Services

P.O. Box 36, 69 Main Street, Stonington, Maine 04681 USA

Tel: 207-367-2200

Email: books@pbp.me

Web: penbaypress.me

Printed in the USA by 360 Digital Books, Madison Heights, Michigan USA

Contents

Preface

This collection of short stories is set circa 1950 in Castine, Maine, although the location could be any of a number of small coastal Maine towns. Some of the writings are based on events related to me by people who lived there at that time, some come from my experience, and the rest are pure fiction. Likewise, the characters are a mix of real and fictional; however the stories and characters describe a way of life that no longer exists here. Physically the town looks much the same now as it did then, but economically and socially there have been many changes. These writings should not be viewed as a nostalgic view, longing for the return to a simpler way of life. There have been many improvements in the lives of those who reside in this area. However, some important things may have been lost in our rush to embrace the modern American way. It is left to you, the reader, to decide if that is true. The author's main hope is that you will enjoy this journey to the Maine coast of seventy years ago.

In Appreciation

The list of people who have helped me with the writing of this book is long and varied. No doubt my memory will omit some who should be on this list, and to them I apologize. I give sincere thanks to them and to those listed here for their help and encouragement.

My late wife, Bary, encouraged me to return to writing after a number of false starts over many years. Her gentle urgings and critiques were basic to the creation of this book.

Virginia Nichols, my high school English teacher, counseled me to major in English with an eye to becoming a writer. I didn't take her advice, but rather followed the lead of the school principal, Jay Caulkins, a mechanical engineer.

In January of 2008 a small group of Castine residents gathered to form a writers group. I was fortunate to be included. It was done under the auspices of the Castine Arts Association, but has been informal to the point of having no officers, no treasury, or even an official name. It has provided the opportunity for members to present their writings to friends who listen and critique. It has been a vital part of progress in my writing. During this time the following persons have participated: Kay Bailey, George Bland, Peter Cooperdock, Barbara-Joy Hare, Brooke Lawsing, Colin Powell, Emma Sweet, Johanna Sweet and Rosemary Wyman.

A number of people, some no longer with us, who lived in Castine during the time of events in this book, recounted and reviewed these stories. They include Edgar Bowden, Betty Bowden Watson, Leland Bowden, Richard Gray, Robert Hall, Harold Hatch, Don Pierce and my siblings: David Small, Mary Whelan and Sylvia Erb. My thanks are extended to all, as the book would not have been possible without their help.

Thank you to Mary Danforth Lozier, Leland Bowden, the Castine Historical Society and the Wilson Museum for permission to print the photographs in this book.

Several illustrations were done by John Gardner and Johanna Sweet. I am most grateful for their willingness to share their artistic abilities. Additional illustrations were done by two artists no longer with us: Richard Danforth and Jay Pratt.

Finally, thank you to my wife, Shelley, for listening to each of these stories and providing encouragement at times when it was needed.

Donald Small
October 2016

The author, 1947, age 9. Photo courtesy of Mary Danforth Lozier

Coppy

Coppy was tired this morning, and the town clock in the church steeple had not yet struck eight. He was always tired recently, and whenever he looked in the mirror an old man who was vaguely familiar peered back at him as if through a fog.

He had worked a variety of jobs in his nearly seventy years, starting when he dropped out of school at fourteen to go on a fishing schooner to Brown's Bank off Nova Scotia. Later he worked in the sardine cannery, mowed lawns, dug ditches, cut pulp wood in the winter, and most recently shoveled and delivered coal. Now, two years after finishing that job, it seemed like there was still black in the wrinkles of his face and hands, and his breathing was labored. He was glad to have left shoveling coal behind, and those monthly Social Security checks, courtesy of Mr. Roosevelt, meant that he didn't really need to find another job, although he had several lawns to care for.

Right now, Coppy was at his usual morning place, the bench

Carrie Connor, with her husband Arthur (Tink), worked as telephone operators and managed the office. Photo courtesy of Castine Historical Society

outside Bob Bowden's barber shop and across from Marion Clark's grocery store, which was in the big brick building. It was a clear May morning with a temperature that hinted at the coming of summer, and Coppy's bench was in the sun. It could be a day of temptation for a spring-fevered school child, so Spunk Hatch, the truant officer, might be busy this afternoon.

Coppy's bench was a good spot to keep track of wayward children and other happenings in downtown Castine, and occasionally someone would stop to talk. To the left of Marion's store was the telephone office where Carrie Connor had just gone in to take the early day shift, relieving her husband, Tink, the night operator. Next to the telephone office was Austin Macomber's store, where one could buy a few basic groceries and beer. Coppy shopped there. The movie theater that Horace Leach and George Coombs owned was directly across Water Street from Macomber's Store. Its real name was The Follies, but it was affectionately

The Follies Theater, circa 1948. Photo courtesy of Leland Bowden

Leach's Garage, circa 1948. Photo courtesy of Castine Historical Society

known as the Tar Paper Palace in reference to its architecture. Coppy liked the movies, a chance to set his own life aside for an hour or two. He collected beer and soda bottles from roadsides and returned them to Macomber's Store for refunds that provided the twenty-five cents admission. Next to the theater was Horace Leach's garage where Chevrolet cars and trucks were sold and serviced. Clarence Gray's son was the mechanic, and Horace's son, Willis, just returned from the Army, also worked there. Mike Perkins' front lawn occupied the space between Leach's garage and the barber shop where Coppy was seated. The barber shop wasn't open yet as Bob, a late riser, didn't get there until nine. But he made up for that by closing early, usually around three in the afternoon. Coppy sometimes wished that he had learned to barber.

To Coppy's right, the Odd Fellows building stood at the corner of Main and Water streets. Robinson's drug store occupied one of the three ground-floor store spaces. Walter, the druggist, usually opened before eight, but neither he nor Mrs. Robinson had arrived yet. Mr. Robinson was a quiet man, always dressed in a gray suit with white shirt and tie. At work he replaced his suit jacket with a white cotton coat that hung down nearly to his knees. Mrs. Robinson, perhaps the boss in the family, was usually behind the soda fountain and not far from the cash register. She was in charge of selling everything in the store except prescriptions: newspapers, magazines, health remedies, postcards and ice cream. The soda fountain was her pride where she prepared a variety of ice cream treats that were served with a smile. Academy students went there for coffee, and they called her "Ma Robinson." However, any young lad who spent too much time looking at a comic book without buying it was subject to a severe reprimand, which was not served with a smile.

Wardwell's Sanitary Market was diagonally across from the drug store. Gus Wardwell had been at work for some time and had just now unlocked the front door. The market was open for the day, and his wife, Algie, would be there soon to help. Fred Wardwell's real estate and insurance office was in the small building just beyond the market. Fred had a successful business, and was pretty much free to come and go as he pleased since Bea Spurling, his one employee, ran the office with great efficiency. To the west of Fred's office stood an old house owned by the Castine Coal Company, the basement of which was used to store coal. Coppy had spent too many unpleasant hours in that basement. Several unoccupied apartments filled the rest of the building. There was too much coal dust for them to be habitable. Next on Water Street was Ma McLeod's American Sailor Restaurant, named for the Academy training ship. Coppy occasionally went there for a supper of meat loaf, mashed potatoes and canned peas, all for eighty-nine cents. If you wanted a roll, that was five cents extra. The last store on the street was Ethel Noyce's shop. She sold sewing supplies, a few clothes and toys. Ethel would arrive shortly, walking down Main Street from the big old house on Murder Alley that she shared with her sister, Grace. She would be wearing a long black dress and pulling a Penobscot Indian pack basket made of ash and with two wheels mounted on the bottom. Ethel, like Marion Clark, had few customers, but kept the store open, perhaps just to have something to do.

Coppy lived in a second-floor apartment in the building across the street from Ethel's store. The first floor was filled with pianos, and the building's owner, Willis Ricker, bought, sold, tuned and played pianos. He also wrote music and many years ago had organized and conducted the Castine Town Band. He loved music. He also had a store on Main Street where he sold newspapers, magazines, candy, and an odd collection of not-very-useful things including sheet music, some of it his. But Coppy liked and admired him. The apartment rent was reasonable, and Coppy could work part of it off by doing odd jobs at the Ricker home on Pleasant Street. Mr. Ricker was Castine's First Selectman, and at one time had been a state legislator.

The lot on the northwest corner of Water and Main streets,

next to Coppy's apartment, was the site of much activity. Alva Clement's crew had torn down the old building that had been there for as long as Coppy could remember and were now putting up a new one. Merton Hooper was relocating his Ford agency garage from Sea Street, the old sardine cannery, to this new building. Merton was getting on in age, and didn't do much at the garage any more, but he came in every day and sat with his feet up on the roll-top desk reading the financial newspaper and keeping track of his stocks. Son Ken was the mechanic, and did most of the other work as well.

Coppy had gone to Marion's store a half hour ago, shortly after she opened. He had been her only customer, buying a small bag of Fig Newtons for his breakfast. They came from one of the glass cookie jars below the bread shelf. Coppy didn't understand why Marion continued with the store, as she had very little to sell, and few customers ever came in to buy any of those things. And, she was even older than Coppy. He supposed it gave her a reason to get out of that huge old house, a series of additions to the main building that years ago she and her late husband operated as the Shattolla Hotel.

As Coppy finished the last Fig Newton, Jimmy Hale's truck pulled into the parking space in front of his bench. Jimmy emerged, went into the store, and soon came out with a bottle of Nesbitt's Orange Soda. He crossed the street and sat next to Coppy. Taking a small pad of paper and a pencil from his shirt pocket, he started to write, then handed the pad to Coppy. It read, "When does drug store open?"

Coppy reached for the pencil in Jimmy's hand and wrote, "Usually eight."

Jimmy looked at the pad, then his pocket watch, grunted, and wrote more. "You working for George Allen?"

Coppy took the pad, read it, and then wrote, "Lawn work and planting flowers. Make enough for beer and movies. You busy?"

"Lots of grass mowing and planting. Building a float for Dr. Pierce's camp."

Coppy had heard about the float for Pierces Pond in Penobscot. The Pierces, summer residents, had been in town during school vacation week, and Jimmy had taken the two boys to get barrels for flotation under the float from Bernard Wardwell. He had started to negotiate a price using his pencil and pad, but that turned out to be a long process, so Jimmy indicated to young Don Pierce that he should do the negotiations. Barnard handed the pad back to Don who, without thinking, started to write. This exchange went through several cycles before either Bernard or Don realized what Jimmy was laughing about. The negotiations finally went into a verbal stage rather than written, and a price was agreed upon.

Jimmy and Coppy carried on a written conversation about when to set out tomato plants and an exchange of jokes while Jimmy finished his soda. He handed the empty bottle to Coppy, got back into his truck and left.

All four members of the Hale family were deaf. They communicated using sign language with those who knew it (very few in Castine), and with paper and pencil for those who didn't. They lived on Court Street in the fine old house that was built by Hale forebears in 1800. They had extensive vegetable gardens and fruit trees on the two acres surrounding the house, and they kept two or three milk cows as well as a flock of chickens. Jimmy worked as a caretaker for several summer residents, his main employers being the Northrop and Pierce families. The two Hale daughters, Hester and Margery, were students at a school for the deaf in Portland, so were home only during the summer and several vacation weeks during the school year.

At eight-thirty, Raymond Bowden rounded the drug store corner and took a seat at the end of Coppy's bench. He was out of breath from walking the four blocks from home and glad for the excuse to stop for a rest. Coppy greeted him with, "Goin' clammin' today, Raymond?"

"I'll give it a try. Low tide's in just a couple a hours, and I'm already late. The tides are not very low for a few days here, so it's not good clammin'."

"Must be a neap tide today."

"A what?"

"Neap tide, neap."

"I don't know about that, but it's not a good clammin' tide."

"Have you started your garden yet, Raymond? It's time to get peas and lettuce and radishes in."

"I've spaded up the garden plot. We don't have a very big one, just some salad things that Irene wants. I wouldn't bother, except she likes it, so all I do is dig it up in the spring. She does the plantin' and weedin'. I don't like messin' 'round in the dirt, rather be in my boat fishin' or on the flats diggin' clams."

"You oughta have a good-size garden, Raymond. You can save a lot of money that way, and it's nice and peaceful workin' in a garden. No one to bother ya, and you don't have to think very hard about what you're doin'. You can just sit there and let your mind wander."

"I'm a salt water man, Coppy. For that matter, this is a salt water town. Always has been. When the Indians lived here, they just came for the summer to fish and dig clams. Did their gardens up north in the spring, then left 'em all summer. Went back in the fall to harvest. Down here they paddled their canoes all over the bay. That's the way I want to live. Maybe I've got some Indian blood in me. Gramp said his grandmother was a Penobscot Indian, so maybe I come by all of that rightly."

"I know what you mean, Raymond, but there's that time when I was with Henry off Dyce's Head, and a squall come up. His boat capsized and we would have drowned if that New Yorker in his yacht hadn't come by to pull us out of the bay. That cured me of wantin' to spend much time in boats."

"Yeah, well, we all take our chances at different things. I'll take mine in my boat, and if I meet my end there, well, that's better than going while sick abed."

Raymond got up, crossed the street, and disappeared down the steps between the brick building and telephone office, a route leading to Sea Street and Dennett's Wharf where he kept his skiff. He was semi-retired, having spent many years as owner and captain of the *Golden Rod*, a steam vessel that carried passengers and mail between Castine, Islesboro and Belfast. When the vessel reached the end of her useful life, she was towed to the middle of the Bagaduce River and sunk. Raymond then turned to clam-digging.

Coppy was pleased with himself for knowing about neap and spring tides and had hoped that Raymond would want him to explain. That hadn't happened, and his thoughts turned to what to do for the rest of the day. The sun disappeared behind a cloud and took with it that hint of summer warmth.

Jake's Boat Shop

Light coming through the windows of Jake Dennett's boat shop was fading early on this cloudy January day, and the three light bulbs suspended from the high ceiling were mostly making shadows rather than throwing light. Jake was immersed in the delicate joinery work of repairing the coaming on *Lucy*, a pretty little sailboat that had been built on Islesboro forty years previous. She had spent the last ten years in a storage building, partially protected from the weather, but leaks in the building's roof had resulted in several areas of rot, and the iron fastenings had rusted badly. The new owner, Hazelton Payson, had brought her to Castine and hired Jake to do a complete rebuild. World War II was over, Hazelton was home from his Navy service, and it was time to get back to some of the finer pleasures of life, like sailing. Jake had put in sister ribs and new garboards, and the planking had been completely refastened with bronze screws to replace the original iron nails. With proper care, *Lucy* should be good for another fifty years.

Jake straightened up from his work and looked toward his assistant. "Time to quit, Ralph. This coamin's lookin' pretty good so far, but I can't see good any more and don't wanna bugger up the final joint."

Ralph, who was repairing the hollow wooden mast, looked at his boss gratefully.

He had spent the previous night playing poker, drinking too much beer, and staying up late. It had been a difficult day, and the idea of quitting work early was very appealing. Sarah had said this morning that they'd have ham steak, fried potatoes and applesauce for supper, his favorite meal. With this cheerful thought in mind he started to put away tools.

"This's a good stoppin' point for me. Got the soft spots in the lower part of the mast replaced. It's time to start scrapin' old varnish off and sandin'."

Jake moved over to Ralph's bench to inspect the work.

"That looks pretty good. Those repair joints are all gonna be below the for'ard deck, so we can still varnish the mast, and the new wood won't show."

"You plan to finish the mast bright?"

"Yeah. Payson wants a nice boat, and he's got the money to pay us right, so we'll varnish the mast, coamings, and oars. Those old oars are perfectly good, but they may be stained so bad that they won't finish good."

"We could paint 'em."

"No, he'd never go for that. He wants lots of bright work... 'spit and polish' he says. Oh, and all the bronze deck fittin's and oar locks need to be cleaned up. I think they're in good shape, just turned green. Why don't you work on those tomorrow mornin', maybe put 'em on the buffin' wheel. Make 'em look like new."

"You don't want me to start varnishin'?"

Joe (left) and Jake (right) Dennett, circa 1950.

Photo courtesy of Castine Historical Society

Ralph's method of work was to finish one job before he started another. Jumping around between two or three different projects was confusing and inefficient.

"No, the shop's too cold this time of year. I'd have to come down here at bedtime to put more wood in the stove, and even with that the fire'd prob'ly be out before we got here in the mornin'."

"How about if I finish scrapin' and sandin' the mast so it's all ready to varnish, then put it up on the rack until warmer weather?"

"Oh... well... yeah, that's a good idea. Yeah, work on that in the mornin'."

"And how about if I scrape and sand those oars too, so they'll be all ready to finish later when I do the mast?"

"Well, see what you can do with 'em. If they don't clean up real good we'll have to get a new pair. But I know Hazelton likes these. They're light and it'll be hard to find new ones with spoon blades... Ah, there's a company in Orono makes nice oars, we can try there if need be. Yeah, work on those oars. You could try some bleach on the bad stains. Sometimes that'll bring the wood back to lookin' almost like new."

Ralph returned to putting away tools while Jake started to sweep shavings and sawdust from the floor. A northeast wind was whistling around the building and blowing into the shop at the window frames. The outside darkness had invaded in spite of the lights, but the glow from the stove showing through the isinglass door and the heat radiating from the stove filled the space with warmth. It gave both occupants a sense of companionship, although neither would ever admit to that. They finished their chores in silence, then donned coats, picked up lunch boxes and started out the door. Just as he was leaving, Jake remembered Nelda's instructions and retrieved a piece of salt cod from where it was hanging on the wall. He put it in his lunch box, locked the shop, and the two trudged up the hill together. Ralph turned right at Water Street, leaning into the wind and snow flurries to walk toward his house at North End. Sarah, ham and fried potatoes were waiting. Jake continued up Main Street, then turned left toward his house on Perkins where his wife Nelda and Bos'n, their black Labrador retriever, would be waiting. Bos'n would make a big fuss over his return.

Nelda and Bos'n

Six o'clock the next morning found Jake in his back yard on the way to the henhouse with a bowl of hot laying mash. Bos'n was making his rounds of the yard to make sure that all was well, and, as usual, peeing on Nelda's lilac bush. Jake hollered at him, but too late. The wind had come around to the northwest sometime in the night, pushing snow clouds out into the Gulf of Maine and bringing with it icy-cold air from Québec. A clear sky and no moon allowed a few stars to show in spite of the morning light in the eastern sky. The rooster was already announcing that another day had started. On entering the henhouse, the eight birds all crowded around Jake's feet, eager for a hot breakfast. Egg production from the hens was way below the warm-weather level, but Jake found three eggs in the laying box. Those, combined with smoked mackerel, leftover cornbread and coffee, would be enough for his and Nelda's breakfast.

Back in the house, Jake loaded the wood box, fed Bos'n his morning ration of kibble, then settled into the rocking chair in front of the Atlantic Clarion kitchen stove. He put his stockinged feet on the warm shelf below the oven door and opened yesterday's copy of the *Bangor Daily News*. He was miffed that the newspaper boy didn't deliver until nearly seven o'clock, which was when he left the house for work. As a result, he read yesterday's news while Nelda fixed breakfast. After thirty years of marriage Jake's contribution to morning conversation was limited.

"Do you want your egg fried or scrambled?"

"Scrambled."

And later, "You want cornbread or toast?"

"Cornbread. What are we havin' for supper?"

"I'll use that fish you brought home last night to make creamed salt cod. We'll have it on baked potatoes, and I plan to make an apple pie today. Those apples we got from the back yard are not very good, and they're almost gone. Maybe you can prune the tree in March. I think it's puttin' all its energy into makin' branches 'stead of apples."

As Jake sat down to his breakfast he allowed that she would have to remind him in March about pruning the tree.

Nelda continued. "Did you know that salt cod was one of George Washington's favorite foods? That and green beans with mushrooms. Read that in my magazine this month."

Jake grunted and wondered where that comment ever came from. It was sometimes difficult to understand what his wife was thinking about.

Nelda was in charge of making sure that their small back yard paid for itself. There was the apple tree, some raspberry bushes, a patch of rhubarb, and a vegetable garden. About half of the latter was devoted to summer crops: tomatoes, cucumbers, spinach, green beans and peas. Some of these were eaten as they ripened, and Nelda canned the rest along with jams and jellies made from the back-yard raspberries, blueberries that she picked behind Fort George in the Tenneys' field, and strawberries she bought from Spunk Hatch. The other half of the garden was used to grow winter vegetables, and these, except for the squash and onions, were stored in the basement to last for a good part of the winter. The squash was put in the pantry where it was warmer and drier; the onions hung over the cellar stairs. And of course there were the chickens.

Every other spring they bought 25 chicks from a mail-order company. By late summer they starting eating the young roosters as fried chicken, and shortly after that the pullets started laying delicious little eggs. As egg production increased, Nelda would take several dozen a week to Wardwell's Sanitary Market, with the proceeds going to reduce their charge account. One rooster would be spared from the fry-pan to head up the new flock of hens and to crow daily at dawn. Both Jake and Nelda liked that sound, although the summer people who came to the neighborhood for July and August did not always appreciate it. During the fall and winter of the second year the old rooster and hens would, one by one, end up in the stew pot for Sunday dinner.

Jake's contribution to the kitchen was fish. During the summer, he caught mackerel, pollock and tomcod from his dock. They ate these several times a week, even though most people in town would not, as the sewer pipes all emptied directly into the Bagaduce River. Jake figured that if the fish was well-cooked, it would be okay, and they never got sick from eating Bagaduce fish. He also went to Smith Cove several times a month for flounder. Some of this, along with mackerel, he smoked for winter use, and once every summer Jake went with several friends down the bay to spend a day fishing for cod and haddock. These would be split, salt-ed and dried in the sun on Dennett's Wharf, then hung up on the shop wall to add to the winter supply of fish. In addition, Raymond Bowden, who dug clams, would occasionally give Jake a "mess" in exchange for letting him keep his rowboat at Dennett's Wharf. Nelda was a champion at knowing what to do with this bounty from the sea. They ate fried fish, baked fish, fish chowder, fish casserole, creamed fish, fried clams, clam fritters, pickled clams, and other dishes that Nelda just made up on the spur of the moment.

Breakfast finished, Jake pulled on another pair of overalls, a second pair of socks, a heavy wool sweater that Nelda had made, and his green rubber boots with felt inserts in the bottom. The boat shop extended out over the river, and the floor was always cold in winter, no matter how warm the air at head level. After years of cold feet, Jake had discovered felt inserts as a way to keep his feet warm. He put on his wool-lined canvas jacket, said goodbye to Nelda, patted Bos'n on the head, and went out through the door for the cold walk to work.

Nelda retrieved the morning paper from the front steps, poured a second cup of coffee, then sat in the rocker to enjoy a half hour of quiet time with the paper. Bos'n lay on the floor by the stove with his chin on Nelda's left foot.

Roy

Jake started his usual route to work along Perkins Street, but when he got to Pleasant he stopped to talk with Roy Bowden who was getting ready to take down Christmas lights from the town tree. The town didn't really own the tree; it grew on the Acadia Hotel lot. The hotel had been torn down several years ago, and the lot was now vacant save for this one magnificent spruce tree. The landowners allowed the town to decorate it for the holiday season, and Roy always volunteered to put the lights up in early December and take them down on the first good day in January.

"Roy, how are you gonna get those lights down? You've got a ten-foot ladder, and the tree must be 50 feet tall."

"Oh, the ladder's just to get me up to the first limb, I climb branches after that."

It was well-known that Roy loved to climb, and the higher and scarier the destination, the more he liked it. Roy, his wife Alice, and their children lived at the top of Dresser Lane, just around the corner from Jake's house. With lots of mouths to feed and jobs as scarce as they were, Roy worked at a variety of occupations. This week he might be a mason building a "chimbley" for the Clergues, next week he might be repairing and painting Dr. North's porch, and after that perhaps installing electrical wiring at the Tenney cottage. He was also the town fire chief, but working as a steeplejack was his very favorite occupation, and he happily painted church steeples from Stonington to Belfast. Jake recalled the story about Harry Small, a deacon at the Congregational church, who told about hiring Roy to paint that steeple. When the job was finished, Roy insisted that Harry climb up to inspect the work. Although not enthusiastic about the prospect of going to that height, he thought it his duty, and agreed. The journey from

The Castine Town Christmas Tree.

Photo courtesy of Castine Historical Society

street level to the top involved squeezing through a twelve-inch-wide door located in the church entry, climbing a ladder that was nothing more than short pieces of board nailed to wall studs, then walking across a narrow plank to the bottom of a second ladder. This led to the sanctuary ceiling level where the ancient town fire alarm mechanism was located, and still another ladder led to the town clock level and the hand-wound mechanism. From here, there was another ladder climb through a trapdoor that emerged next to the church bell. Roy had removed a louvered panel to allow access to a narrow outside ledge. Harry made it as far as this ledge, then realized that the path continued up an old wooden ladder that had been tied to the steeple and, above that, pieces of board were nailed to the steeple all the way to the base of the weather vane. When Roy suggested that he continue to climb, Harry declined, saying he could see perfectly well from there that Roy had done an excellent job. He was, however, puzzled about the fresh coat of paint on the weather vane. It was mounted on a steel rod that extended perhaps four feet above the steeple, and it pierced a bowling-ball-size sphere between the steeple and vane. It seemed to be completely out of reach.

"Roy, how did you get the weather vane down to paint it, and how did you get it back up again?"

"Oh, I didn't take it down. That was the best part of all. You see, I climbed up those boards nailed to the steeple all the way to the top. Now, when you get there you reach up as high as you can and grab the rod above that ball. You give a good jump off the last board and just wrap your legs around the rod and sit on the ball. Then you can reach the weather vane. I just carried along a wire brush, paint brush, and a can of Rustoleum. Sat up there for a couple of hours. Beautiful clear day... I could see forever... Camden Hills, Mt. Desert Island, and, you know, when I looked directly east, I could see Spain. They was havin' a bullfight. You want to go up and see?"

Harry declined, saying he had to get back to work.

Jake realized that he, too, needed to be on the way to work, but he stayed to watch Roy take some tools from the back of his '39 Dodge pickup truck, walk across the field, climb the ladder, and pull himself branch to branch toward the top of the tree. Jake shook his head and, although not a religious man, made what amounted to a silent prayer that Roy wouldn't fall off the top. He then headed down Pleasant and rounded the corner onto Water Street. As he passed Ethel Noyes' shop he could see that downtown Castine was early-morning quiet. Several people, visible through the big window of the American Sailor Restaurant, were having coffee, and Gus Wardwell was just unlocking the door to Wardwell's Sanitary Market.

Gus

Gus looked up from unlocking the market door and saw Jake walking toward him on Water Street. Gus waved, knowing that Jake would not return it, but he did get a nod. Jake was... what was the word? Taciturn. Gus remembered that word from a high school vocabulary lesson and thought he knew lots of taciturn people.

This was Gus's usual arrival time of seven fifteen. It was forty-five minutes before the store opened and allowed some time for Gus to do chores without being interrupted by customers. The first job was to tend the coal furnace in the cellar. Gus descended the steep stairs very carefully. He had fallen on them a few years ago, and, though not seriously hurt, he realized that the next time his luck might not hold. He switched on the light at the bottom and did a swift visual check to see that all was in order. The basement was divided by a partition, and the space at the bottom of the stairs was empty save for two large wooden barrels set upright, each with a hand pump on top. One held vinegar, the other molasses. These were for customers who brought gallon jugs to the store for Gus to fill here in the cellar. But now, on through a door in the partition to the furnace room. Here was the big, old, cast iron hot-air furnace that heated the building and a bin next to it that was nearly full of anthracite coal. Gus had stoked the furnace well the night before and closed the air for a slow burn, so there was still a good bed that was ready for a few shovelfuls of coal this morning. What a pleasure it was having a coal furnace rather than dealing with firewood. Then it was back upstairs to sweep the floor and dust the most obvious horizontal surfaces. Next, check the meat locker and do a bit of trimming of dried edges on the beef hanging there. Then, open the safe under the counter to retrieve money to stock the cash register and, finally, unlock the front door.

There were usually few customers before nine o'clock which was when Algie got there, but this morning Esther Perkins arrived shortly after eight. She wanted eggs, a jar of mayonnaise, loaf of bread, and a pound of hamburg. Gus went to the meat locker, cut several chunks of round beef, and ran them through the meat grinder. It weighed in at just exactly one pound. Gus was good at that. In the meantime, Esther had gotten the mayonnaise and bread.

"Now then, Mrs. Perkins," Gus asked, "do you want hen eggs or chicken eggs?"

Esther humored him. "I've eaten enough hen eggs recently and would like chicken eggs for a change."

Gus chuckled, got the eggs from the meat locker, rang up the prices on the cash register, and put her purchases in a paper bag.

"That'll be a dollar eighty-five."

Esther gave him two one-dollar bills and received the change along with the comment, "You be careful walkin' home. The streets are treacherous in places."

So began another day for Gus at Wardwell's Sanitary Market. He worked at the store five days a week from early morning to late afternoon, plus Saturday mornings, and had been doing it for thirty years. All of that store time, plus the usual variety of chores to be done at home on Green Street, left precious little time for other interests, but he did have one hobby. No, more than a hobby, a passion. Gus loved to build and race boats, hydroplanes to be specific. They were tiny craft, eight feet long and just shy of four feet wide, with a cockpit big enough for one person to squeeze into in a kneeling position. They were built of quarter-inch plywood with a very light framework inside, the whole boat weighing less than a hundred pounds. A steering wheel at the front of the cockpit was connected by cables to an outboard engine hanging on the transom. The engine of choice was a 9.9 horsepower Mercury. Gus had heard that an engine with 10 horsepower or more was taxed at a high rate, thus the 9.9 figure. And that engine would make a prop-

Main Street, Castine, circa 1950. Wardwell's Market on the left.
Photo courtesy of Wilson Museum

erly designed and constructed hydroplane go like blazes. Driving it was the most exciting experience Gus could imagine.

But that part would have to wait till summer. Winter was construction time for the newest version of a Gus Wardwell hydroplane, and he enjoyed this almost as much as racing. The first boat, which he had built four years ago, was from a plan he ordered from *Popular Mechanics Magazine*. That one worked reasonably well, but Gus identified several areas in the design that needed improvement. So the next year he built the second boat, similar to the first, but with modifications that resulted in noticeably improved speed and control. And each year since then, a newly designed hydroplane that performed even better than the last version emerged from Gus' carpenter shop. This year was to be no exception. Gus found time to spend several evenings each week and perhaps Sunday afternoon in his shop. It was a lovely time. He took great pride in the shop being neat and clean. There was a place for every tool, and every tool was in its place except when being used. Each tool was clean and oiled, and all the cutting edges were sharp. Lumber was stored in overhead racks and sorted according to size and variety. The shop was filled with the scent of wood shavings, mainly a mix of cedar and pine. Currently, the framework of the new boat sat on a jig in the center of the shop, and Gus had set a goal of refining this part of the construction process to result in reducing the weight and improving the workmanship. He was succeeding. The framework was noticeable lighter than last year's, the joints fit exactly right, there were no glue runs, all pieces were sanded, and the result was as good as a fine piece of furniture. Cutting out plywood pieces was the next step, and Gus hoped to find time to start that tonight. He also had to come up with a name for the boat, although every one so far had been christened *Algie*. His wife liked that. She was flattered that after all these years her husband would name his pride and joy after her. And he liked it because when he was driving he could tell *Algie* what to do and she did it.

That afternoon after work, Gus went to his shop and sat on a stool, staring at the bones of his new boat. He started to lose himself in racing thoughts. There was only one real race a year in which he participated—Fourth of July in Castine harbor. He had won this three of the past four summers, the one loss being last year. That had been close to a disaster. Gus was in the lead, approaching the third buoy in Smith Cove, when he swerved to avoid a floating log. This sudden turn, combined with the slight wake of a distant lobster boat, had resulted in his hydroplane flipping over. Gus ended up in the water, unhurt save for his pride. Jake Dennett was nearby in his power launch with a boatload of sightseers. He pulled Gus from the water, righted *Algie*, and towed her back to the town dock. All of this was terribly embarrassing, but the worst part was the fuss people made over it. It was weeks before Gus could speak to someone and they not bring up this subject. But the Fourth of July race, along with joy rides by himself and occasional impromptu races with anyone who brought a hydroplane to Castine on a Saturday afternoon, were enough to maintain his enthusiasm. As these thoughts descended on him, his view of the shop faded, and he found himself on the float at the town dock on a fine summer's day....

> Almost no wind. The river is like a mirror save for a few ripples. The newest *Algie*, just launched, is there in the water beside the float, and his grandson, Wayne, is holding her firmly in place while Gus dons his life vest and crawls over the edge into the cockpit. He arranges his feet and legs as best he can, then twists his body to

reach the engine. Set the throttle to start, squeeze the fuel line bulb, put the engine in neutral, pull the choke knob, then yank the starting cord. The engine springs to life. Wayne releases *Algie* and pushes her out into the tidal current. Gus eases the engine into forward, then pushes the throttle ahead slightly for a test run at low speed. All seems well. No water leaks, she's already up on an easy plane, and *Algie* seems eager for more speed. Gus pushes the throttle farther ahead, and still farther, until finally the engine is wide open. Gus and *Algie* are flying over the water surface toward Smith Cove. The wind and spray are in his face, the engine noise is deafening, and the boat is pounding on water ripples. Man and boat have become a single living being. It is exhilarating, stupendous. It is the experience that will last through all of those long, cold winter days....

Suddenly Gus was back in his shop. Algie was at the door. "What are you doing? Have you lost track of time? Supper's been ready for ten minutes, and I can tell you're not making any progress on that boat anyway."

Gus smiled and followed Algie back to the house.

George

The next morning, Gus arrived at the market and started his usual chores. When he got to the bottom of the cellar stairs and flipped the light switch, the bulb did a final glorious burst of light, then all went dark. Gus went back up the stairs to the shelf where light bulbs were kept, but it was nearly empty. There were twenty-five watt bulbs only, and he needed at least sixty watts for light in the basement.

"Hmmm... Not good, will have to go see George for more, but he doesn't open till eight... after Algie gets here then."

Gus talked to himself when no one else was around. In the meantime he retrieved a flashlight from the shelf under the cash register, and took it to the cellar for light to tend the furnace.

George was the proprietor of Coombs Hardware Store, the first business on the left coming down Main Street when entering the downtown area. He had an amazing assortment of hardware items considering the small size of the store. Shelves lined the walls from floor to ceiling and filled the center of the store as well, leaving narrow aisles. Common hardware items were visible and easily accessible by the customer, but if an unusual item were requested, say a replacement valve assembly for a thirty-year-old Universal hand water pump, George would hesitate for just a few seconds, then get a stepladder, climb to a top shelf near the back of the store, and produce just the valve needed.

George was not only the proprietor of the store, he was also the only clerk, so, like Gus, he spent long hours there five and a half days every week. He closed the store for one week in spring when he and Edith went on a road trip with their Ford sedan, pulling the house trailer they had purchased in 1936. He and Harry Small had set themselves up as dealers for Caravan Travel Trailers, and each family had purchased one at wholesale price. No other trailers were ever ordered by this partnership.

There were far fewer customers for the hardware store than for Wardwell's Market, thus George spent more time waiting. He had solved this problem by starting an electrical appliance repair business. A workbench behind the sales counter was the center for fixing toasters, lamps and radios. Ah, radios. Radios were to George as hydroplanes were to Gus. He loved them. George was a ham operator, meaning he had a shortwave radio station and used it to talk with friends all around the world, friends he had never seen but still knew as well as any of his Castine neighbors. The radio was also used during the winter when the Maritime Academy training cruise was in progress. George invited family members of the crew to come to his house to talk with their loved ones on the ship. Wives and children soon learned to press the button on the microphone before speaking, to say "over" and release the button at the end of the message, and to not interrupt in the middle of an incoming message. It was an exciting and much-appreciated service for these families.

Shortly after Algie arrived at the market, Gus walked up Main Street to Coombs Hardware Store where he saw George at his repair bench probing the open back of a parlor model Emerson radio. Vacuum tubes, wires, other unknown electrical items plus papers were spread out on the bench.

"Mornin', George."

George, absorbed in his work, had not heard Gus enter and jumped slightly at the greeting,

"Oh, hello, Gus. I didn't hear you come in. What can I do for ya?"

George put down his screwdriver and changed from radio repairman to store clerk.

"Well, I need a package of sixty-watt light bulbs for the store, then a box of three-quarter inch number 6 galvanized wood screws and a quart of exterior primer paint for my boat."

Gus kept two charge accounts with George, one for the store, the other for his woodworking shop. As George set out to retrieve the three items, Gus said, "I see you've hired that Bowden boy to do some jobs around here."

"Yep, he's done some painting inside, and he's cleaned out a bunch of junk that's accumulated in the basement. Things I'd intended to do, but just haven't gotten around to. It's good to get 'em done."

"There's a rumor about some trouble you had with him."

"Trouble? No, I haven't had any trouble. He's a good worker, and smart as a whip. I thought he might need a little guidance though, and hiring him gives me a chance to try that—plus it gets those jobs done."

George put the items in a paper bag, and Gus, with his purchases, went out the door and down the street. He waited for Jimmy Hale to drive past before crossing to the market.

What George had not mentioned was what some people might consider to be "trouble."

Several weeks previous, he had noticed one morning that the new display box of jackknives, which he had set out on the sales counter just before closing the day before, was now missing one knife. He looked around to see if there were any other obvious missing items, and the only possibility was a rack near the counter that held small flashlights. There were two where he thought there should be three. George pondered this during the day, and there seemed to be no conclusion other than that someone had come into the store during the previous night.

George went home a bit earlier than usual. Edith was working at the library until mid-evening, but had left a macaroni casserole for his supper. George put it in the oven, then read the *Bangor Daily News* while waiting for it to heat. After eating, he wrote a

"February Street." Painting by Richard Danforth, 1952. Coombs' Hardware at far left.
Courtesy of Wilson Museum

note saying that he had some work to catch up on at the store, and would be home later. George left the note at Edith's place at the table, put on his boots and coat, then left to cross the field to the back door of his store.

There was only a light layer of snow on the ground, so the walking was easy, and there was enough moonlight that he did not need the flashlight that was in his pocket. Arriving at the back door, he got it out to better see the keyhole, and when he turned it on, noticed that there were footprints in the snow other than his. Strange, he had not used this door for several weeks. Before turning the key, he checked to see that the door was locked. It was. Perhaps someone else had a key. George entered the store, relocked the door behind him, and wended his way through the aisles to the sales counter using the flashlight rather than turning on store lights. Nothing seemed to be amiss, and it was very quiet. The street was quiet. It seemed like the whole town was deserted, and he mumbled to himself, "This is probably a dumb thing to be doing, but I guess it's worth a try."

He settled into the old armchair that was squeezed in next to the repair bench. Edith had evicted it from the living room, saying it was worn out and ratty-looking, but George liked the chair and had brought it to the store rather than taking it to the dump. It was supposed to be a place to sit while reading electrical repair manuals, but right now he had no light, so couldn't read anything. Instead, he settled into a mental planning process on how to reorganize his ham radio room to make space for some new equipment. The minutes went by, then an hour, and the store remained very quiet. Then, at about six forty-five, there was a sound from the back. Outside? Yes. Someone talking, not very loud, but not George's imagination either. He slowly got up from the chair and felt his way through an aisle to the side of the store where he could reach the switch to the store lights and where he could dimly see the back door. There were two people talking. Men? Maybe, or boys. Nervous laughter mixed in with the talking. He suddenly realized his only weapon was the four-cell flashlight in his hand, and he had no idea what the next few minutes would bring. He waited for the door to move. It didn't; rather the transom window above it slowly lowered down to where it hung vertical, then two legs appeared, a body followed, and the figure dropped to the floor. George flipped the light switch, and there stood the young thief, his mouth hanging open. There were rapid footsteps from behind the store of the second person running off.

"Well, Edgar, so you're the one been comin' in here after closin' time."

Edgar, shaking with fear, was sure that George would call the sheriff, and he would end up in reform school.

"I... I've only been here once before."

"Well, this makes two times too many, doesn't it."

"Y-yes, sir, I guess it does."

"Why did you do it? Need that jackknife, but didn't have the money?"

"No, sir, I didn't need it. I'm sorry I took it, and there was a flashlight, too."

"Well, the knife costs a dollar eighty-nine, and the flashlight is two and a quarter. You need to pay me for those, or bring them back if they're still in new condition."

"Yes, sir. I'll pay you for them. I've used the knife, and Phi..., uh, the flashlight got dropped. It's dented."

"Who's your friend who helped out?"

"Oh, he didn't really do anything. I just convinced him to come along."

"Okay, if that's how you want to leave it, but both of you need to know that this business of breaking into a store and stealing things is absolutely wrong. If you continue like that, you're going to have a very sorry life."

"I know. I'll never do it again, I promise."

"You tell your friend that, too. Now come over to the counter, and I'll tell you what's going to be done about this."

Edgar was scared. He could feel sweat running from his forehead and into his eyes. It stung. He was sure that a call to the sheriff would be next. George went behind the sales counter, reached into a drawer, and produced a key. He handed it to Edgar.

"This is a key to the front door. In the future, if you need somethin' here after the store is closed, you use the key and come in through the front door. Sneakin' in through the back is no good. Now, whatever it is that you take, write it down on this pad of paper along with the price, and the next day you come in and pay me for it. Do you understand that?"

"Yes, sir."

"I'm putting a huge amount of trust in you, and I fully expect you to live up to it. Understood?"

Edgar nodded, hardly able to believe what George had just said.

"Alright, now you leave through the front door and go straight home. You must have schoolwork to do."

"Yes sir, I do. And thank you so much. Are you going to tell my mother?"

"Not for now. I'll see how this works out."

As they started toward the door, George had one more idea to try.

"Edgar, do you have time to work here at the store after school? I've got a number of things that need doing, and I just don't seem to find the time to get 'em done."

"I'd like that, but we've got basketball practice after school every day. I could come Saturday mornin's."

George said that would be fine, then reached out his right hand. Edgar did the same and remembered his grandfather's advice to always give a firm handshake.

Sylvia's Boston Trip

The Big Ben alarm clock broke the early morning stillness of the sleeping house on Main Street. Sylvia peered out from under the covers to look at it—five o'clock. She was momentarily confused about why the early waking, but then remembered: her April college vacation was over. It was time to return to Boston for a few more months of study and then graduation as a member of the class of 1946. She had to be in Bangor to catch the nine fifteen train. Dad would drive her to Union Station, but had to be back in Castine by eight o'clock for his work, thus a very early departure from home and the prospect of a long wait in Bangor. She pulled herself out of bed, put on a robe, and opened the window shade only to be struck by the sight of... snow! How could that be? Yesterday was warm and sunny, daffodils were in bloom, the lawn was green, and she had spent the afternoon with Mother cleaning out flower beds. It was supposed to be spring.

Sylvia dressed, put a final few things in her suitcase, and carried it downstairs where Mother had prepared a breakfast of oatmeal, toast from her homemade bread, coffee and an orange. Table talk was all about snow (there were more than four inches of it out there) and what the driving would be like for the trip to Bangor.

Dad and Sylvia were in the car and on the way before six and found themselves on a trackless road. The snowplow for the town truck had been put away for the season a week ago, and there was no sign of the state truck that normally plowed Route 166. It was a slow trip, but they had no real problems until arriving at Hardscrabble Hill. There were several cars and pickup trucks at the bottom, and no one was having luck in getting up that hill. Dad took his turn at a try, but the 1940 Chevrolet would go no farther than a quarter of the way, so they turned around and started back toward Castine.

As he drove, Dad had an idea for an alternate way to get to Boston. Captain Arthur Ladd's mail boat, *Hippocampus*, would be leaving for Belfast at about nine, and he carried passengers. Sylvia could take the mail boat, then walk to the Belfast train station, which was just a few blocks from the pier, and get the late-morning passenger train. With that settled, the conversation turned to the possibility that they would have to leave the car at the bottom of Neck Hill and walk home, but when they got to Marsh Bridge, the road had been cleared and sanded. Apparently Mack Wardwell had put the plow back on the town truck and was now clearing streets. The travelers were home with time for coffee and toast before Dad walked over to the Academy where he worked. Soon after, Sylvia walked down Main Street carrying her suitcase and lunch box in which Mom had packed a ham sandwich, an oatmeal cookie and a thermos of hot tea.

The entrance to the mail boat building had been cleared of snow, and Sylvia walked through the main part, a storage area, to a small office at the water end of the building. The room had a rolltop desk in one corner covered with piles of paper, a pot-bellied stove, several chairs, and shelves on one wall that held cans of paint, rope, shackles and other boat items. The smell of the rope filled the room. A single window faced the pier and Bagaduce River. At the end of the pier a loading ramp that pivoted at the inboard end could be adjusted as the tide changed to bring the outer end to the level of the boat's deck. This simplified the process of loading cargo and provided easy access for passengers to board. Sylvia found the office empty of people, but warmed by the stove. Through the window she could see Mr. Gray, mate on the boat, shoveling a path to the end of the pier, and Capt. Ladd carrying two mailbags toward the *Hippocampus*. He soon returned to the office and was surprised to find Sylvia there, but said he would be glad to take her to Belfast. The one-way ticket cost a dollar and ten cents, and they'd leave in about a half hour. Sylvia waited next to the stove, seated on an old wooden chair that was slightly rickety and spattered with paint. At nine o'clock she was aboard the mail boat, and they were leaving the dock.

The vessel's cabin was small, and the middle was piled high with boxes and mail bags, but there were benches along both sides for passengers. Sylvia took a cushioned seat next to the woodstove. It was a cozy place to start the trip, but the stove was new and emitted a foul, smoky odor.

Snow had finally stopped falling, and what had been a breeze earlier in the morning had now turned into a serious southwest wind. *Hippocampus* tossed and rolled in response to the waves coming across Penobscot Bay. By the time they cleared Dyce's Head, Sylvia was feeling very uncomfortable. Her stomach seemed to be rolling with a motion that was just opposite that of the boat. A short time later Capt. Ladd, noticing his passenger's complexion, brought her a bucket.

"We won't tell your father about this," he said, knowing that Dad, Lt. Cdr. Small, was retired Navy and a licensed merchant mariner. "And you might feel better if you came forward with me and stood by the wheel. If fact, I'll let you steer if you want. Doing something and being able to see the horizon will make you feel better."

"I've never steered a boat before. I don't know how."

"Well, it's time you learned. Here's your opportunity. You come up here now."

Sylvia went forward and stood at the wheel of the *Hippocampus*. Capt. Ladd, standing beside her, said, "You see that point of land just to the left of where we're headed?" Sylvia nodded. "Well, that's the north end of Islesboro, Turtle Head. We'll keep

Captain Arthur Ladd (right) in 1952 at his retirement party. Postmaster Charles Richardson stands on the dock with him, while crowds of well-wishers can be seen in the background. Photo courtesy of Castine Historical Society

goin' in that direction 'til we get past Islesboro, then just a slight turn to port will take us right into Belfast harbor. You know what direction port is?"

Sylvia nodded. "I know about port and starboard."

"Good. And steering is just like a car. You turn the top of the wheel in the direction you want the boat to go. The next thing is, that instrument right in front of you is the compass. It tells what direction the boat is headed. The number that's right in front of that black line is... 290 degrees, that's our compass heading, and that's what we want to follow, although now you can keep the visual heading. If it was foggy or dark, we'd just have the compass heading to follow. That's a little scary at first when you're running at night, but with some experience, you get to trust the compass, and it works fine."

Sylvia soon felt comfortable with this new skill of steering a boat, and actually enjoyed it. The bucket was not put to use, and as they rounded Turtle Head she changed course slightly, heading for Belfast harbor.

"Where did the name *Hippocampus* come from? Is that some kind of animal like a hippopotamus?"

"What?" Capt. Ladd was absorbed in reading the *Bangor Daily News*, an article about the Red Sox. "Oh, yeah, something like that. Your father knows Greek, and if you asked him, he'd tell you that it's the Greek word for seahorse. And it's a good name. She's a fine sea boat, and she's strong and reliable like a horse. She'll be good to you as long as you take care of her."

"You must have owned it for a long time, as long as I can remember."

"Yep, I've had her for nearly fifteen years now, but she's a lot older than that. Built in 1913 down in New York for the Porter family. They're the ones that own Great Spruce Head Island and come there summers. Elliot Porter's a son. I'm told he's a famous photographer. Originally, of course, she was a luxury yacht, lots of varnished mahogany and polished brass. Looked a lot different then. You can see some of the brass is still here, but I don't get around to polishing much, so it's turned green or painted over."

"So you bought *Hippocampus* from the Porters?"

"Yes, they owned her nearly twenty years, but the government took her over during World War I. The Navy used her as a patrol boat here in Penobscot Bay. Had a machine gun mounted on the bow, and supposedly they were looking for German submarines. Never found any."

"We're getting close to Belfast, and I'm just headed for the middle of the harbor. Is that okay?"

"You're doing fine. Just be aware of that buoy coming up. It's red, and the rule is red-right-return. We're going into the harbor, or returning, so you keep the buoy on your right. And when you finish college, if you want a job driving a boat, come see me."

Sylvia disembarked *Hippocampus* at the Belfast pier, and walked five minutes to the train station. The Belfast and Moosehead Lake train comprised a steam engine, a tender filled with coal and water, three box cars, a flat bed car loaded with scrap metal, an ancient wooden passenger car, and a caboose. It left the station at eleven thirty with Sylvia one of only four people in the passenger car. There was a woodstove for warmth, which was tended by the conductor who occasionally appeared from the caboose. Rows of empty wooden seats lined both sides of the car, and two kerosene lanterns, hanging from the ceiling, swung as the train rumbled along the track. Sylvia felt sufficiently better from the boat trip that she opened her lunch box and ate the cookie and drank a cup of tea. The sandwich could wait. The trip from Belfast to Burnham Junction took just over an hour, and included several stops along the way to pick up freight items that were loaded into one of the box cars. The "Junction" was just that—the intersection of several rail lines and sidings along with a rail-side platform and freight office, but no passenger waiting room. Sylvia found a bench on the platform outside the freight office, and was thankful that the sun was appearing through breaks in the clouds. The snow was rapidly melting. She sat there with her feet on the suitcase, lunch box in her lap, eating the ham sandwich while waiting for the Boston and Maine train. Tea from the thermos was still hot and tasted wonderful on this blustery day.

It was nearly two in the afternoon when the train finally appeared, and to Sylvia's relief, it stopped so that she could board. She bought her ticket from the conductor and found a comfortable seat for the ride to Boston.

All signs of daylight were gone when they arrived at North Station, and there was no sign of snow there. There were taxis, however, many of them lined up outside the station. Sylvia took one for the final leg of her trip and arrived at her dormitory at eight in the evening. She paid the taxi driver and included a ten cent tip, then climbed the three flights of stairs to her room. As she entered, her roommate looked up from a book.

"Where have you been? I thought you'd be here hours ago."

Sylvia set her suitcase down on her bed, put the lunch box on her bureau, then turned the chair at her desk so it faced Sarah and sat. "Let me tell you about my day."

Notes:

Information about the *Hippocampus* came from an article, "The fall and rise of the *Hippocampus*" by Steve Cartwright, published in the April 2010 issue of *Points East*. That article went on to describe the continuing life of *Hippocampus*. Capt. Ladd sold her in 1952, and since then she has been a University of Maine research vessel and a tuna-fishing vessel. More recently she fell into disrepair and had the look of a derelict ready to be demolished. Fortunately that did not happen, and the new owner is pursuing a complete restoration, due for completion in 2016. Hopefully *Hippocampus* will once again cruise Penobscot Bay.

The Belfast and Moosehead Lake Railroad started operations in 1870 as a freight and passenger line between Belfast and Burnham Junction. The original plan was to extend the track to Moosehead Lake, but that never occurred. By 1990, freight operations had ceased, but the line continued as a tourist attraction excursion train until 2008 when financial problems forced the closing of that operation. However, the Brooks Preservation Society has recently acquired the line and is running weekend excursions during the summer and fall. So this venerable train is once again part of the Penobscot Bay area.

A Job for Leland

Freshman algebra class was held in the second floor north-facing room of Abbott School, and Leland currently had the seat closest to the back window. He was trying to ignore the warm October day on the other side of that window and concentrate on the blackboard contents: $x = y^2+4$. Mr. Kassay circled it and turned to face the class, pointing at a person in the front row.

"Mary, if *x* equals y squared plus four, and we need to know what *y* equals, what is the first step we take?"

Mary, generally considered by her classmates to be the smartest in their group, paused for just three seconds, and responded, "Subtract four from both sides of the equal sign."

Leland would not have known what to say had he been called on, but Mary's answer did make sense, and he even knew the next step: take the square root of both sides.

Mr. Kassay waved the chalk above his head. "That's right, Mary. Now, what's the next step? Who knows the answer?" Leland was one of several to put his hand up, even wagging it a bit, hoping to be called on, but Mr. Kassay pointed at Alice, who said, "Subtract *x* from both sides?" Leland slumped in his chair. Alice always tried hard, but was not in the same league as Mary, or Leland for that matter. The teacher, not wanting to discourage his pupil, said, "You could do that, but it wouldn't really get us any closer to the answer. What about taking the square root of both sides?"

Mr. Kassay turned to the board, flourished his chalk, and started to write this step of the solution. Just at that moment Leland glanced out the window, and his eye caught movement in the yard next door. Burt Stover was repairing the door to the shed behind Mrs. Ames' house. His dog Lucy had apparently found something of interest under the shed. She was barking and digging furiously in the flower garden next to the building. Soil and plants were spewing out onto the lawn. All thoughts of algebra fled from Leland's mind as he watched a skunk squeeze out from under the shed. Burt, wondering what Lucy was up to, left his job and came around the corner just in time to see the skunk send a stream in the dog's direction. It was a direct hit just below her jaw. The skunk waddled off toward the alder patch beyond the shed, while Lucy rolled in the grass, having lost all interest in pursuit. As Leland covered his mouth to keep from laughing, he realized that Mr. Kassay was calling his name.

"Leland? Would you care to tell the rest of the class what it is that you find to be so amusing? Or you could start by giving your answer to the question."

Leland tried to bring his mind back to algebra class, but could only think, "Question? What question?" He stammered, "I-I'm sorry, Mr. Kassay, I didn't hear what the question was."

Normally, Leland might be sent to the principal's office now to be disciplined, but since Mr. Kassay was the principal, it all happened right there.

Leland in the classroom. Drawing by Johanna Sweet

"Well, why didn't you hear the question? I stated it with perfect clarity. Leland, whatever's going on outside is not important right now. You need to pay attention to what's going on in here. It's the important..." Mr. Kassay droned on, and Leland was thoroughly embarrassed to be scolded with all of his classmates listening. Furthermore, he had lost all interest in what the value of y might be. How was that going to help him build a hen house?

The bell finally sounded, indicating the end of algebra class, and Leland moved to the adjacent room for the last hour of the day, English. Mrs. Wardwell, his favorite teacher, was the subject of Leland's most recent poem, although he had not found the courage to show it to her yet.

I used to hate my English class with literature and rule,
Until our Mrs. Wardwell came to our little school.
She made me see the sunny side of studying each day.
She's been here most a year now. I hope she's here to stay.
(Poem courtesy of Mr. Leland Bowden)

Basketball practice was held every day after school at the town hall. At three twenty Leland joined Joe Hackett and Linney (his mother called him Linwood) Gray as they walked across the Common and along Court Street toward Emerson Hall. Linney had news that put basketball talk aside.

"My father says his fur dealer is paying fifty cents for a skunk pelt, and there's lots of skunks in town this fall. He thinks that someone could trap thirty or forty of 'em if they tried. That'd be around twenty dollars. Dad says he'll teach me how to skin 'em and what to do with the pelts."

"I saw a skunk just this afternoon. Came out from under Mrs. Ames' garden shed and squirted Burt Stover's dog. I bet he was some mad. I bet both of 'em was mad."

Linney, frowning, looked at Leland for a moment, then said, "How about if the three of us start a trappin' business and specialize in skunks?"

"Can we borrow traps from your father?"

"He doesn't have any the right size, but we can buy some at Rice and Miller's for two dollars apiece. I think two traps would be enough. Anybody got money? You can get it back after we start catchin' skunks."

"I haven't got any."

"I picked up soda and beer bottles last Saturday, but only got twenty-four cents. And I've already spent five cents of that. We could ask around and see if anyone else has traps we could borrow—maybe Spunk Hatch."

The boys, having arrived at Emerson Hall, raced in through the front door and up the stairs to the second-floor auditorium which comprised a large open floor with a stage at the front and balcony at the rear. It was used for public meetings, music and theater events, and high school basketball. The floor was laid out with markings for basketball games: center line, foul lines, out-of bounds, etc., but the size was not that of a regulation basketball court. The width was reasonably close, but the distance between baskets was too short. Further, an overhead beam was low enough that it obstructed shots to the basket from one side. These problems, however, were typical of other nearby towns as well, and the players learned to deal with them. This afternoon's practice concentrated on passing and dribbling for the freshmen, many of whom were new to the game. Older students worked on foul shots and lay-ups, and then at four thirty Mr. Savage talked to the boys about sportsmanship and fair play.

Leland, home on State Street by five o'clock, was pleased to find his older brother, Ormy, his wife Margaret, and their baby joining the family for supper. After everyone was seated and starting the meal, Ormy announced that he had news.

"I've got a job up in Aroostook County, close to Sherman

Mills, workin' the potato harvest. I'm leavin' on Thursday, and be gone about a month, more or less. It depends on weather and how long it takes to finish the harvest."

Mother looked at Ormy. "What about Margaret and the baby? Are they going, too?"

Margaret responded for him. "No, we're staying. There's no place for us to live up there. They've got a bunk house for the workers, and they feed them, but no place for families. We'll be okay here."

Dad wondered what kind of a job it was. "Are you pickin' potatoes, or what?"

"I'll be drivin' a truck. You know, up in the County, the kids get out of school for potato harvest time, and they do a lot of the actual pickin'. That is, they dig the potatoes out of the ground and put 'em in barrels. I'll be drivin' a truck along the rows and puttin' the barrels in the back, then goin' to the potato barn and unloadin' 'em. I'll be gettin' a dollar an hour, and they say I'll be workin' ten, twelve hours a day, six days a week. That money'll give us a pretty good start on gettin' through the winter."

It was 1933, and jobs everywhere, including this coastal Maine town, were scarce. He looked at Margaret, smiled, then reached over and took the baby from her arms. He still found it hard to believe that at twenty-one he was a father. This new responsibility was a bit scary, but the baby had stolen his heart, just as Margaret had. He was determined to do whatever necessary to care for them.

Mother was listening, but her mind was still on family matters. "Margaret, will you be going to stay with your folks? We'd love to have you stay here while Ormy's gone."

"No, I'm going to stay at our home. Ormy's fixed most of the things that were wrong with the house, and I'll ask my dad to stop by every day or two. The worst thing right now is there's a skunk livin' under the house, and I hope he'll be gone by Thursday. Ormy traded Norwood Bakeman one of his clam rakes for a trap just to catch the skunk."

"Skunk trap?" Leland took a sudden interest in the conversation and turned to Ormy. "How about if you let me tend the trap and catch your skunk, and in return let me use the trap while you're gone?"

"I'll do better than that. I'll give you the trap if you'll cut firewood for Margaret. You'll need to come over at least once a week, and it'll prob'ly take a few hours, but there's two ash trees that blew over last year right near the house. I've been cuttin' firewood out of them. There's an ax, a saw and a wheelbarrow in the shed behind the house. How about it?"

"Sounds good to me. I'll be over Saturday mornin'."

On Saturday Leland woke to the sound of rain beating hard on his bedroom window. Not a good time to cut wood, so after breakfast he helped Dad sharpen lawnmowers and put up two shelves in the back entry. Soon after lunch the rain had slacked off, and the sky in the west was bright. The afternoon would be fine for cutting wood, but he'd wait a few hours hoping for things to dry a bit. At two o'clock Margaret's father stopped by with a dollar bill for Leland. He had been to Margaret's, and she needed flour, sugar and baking powder. Would Leland be willing to get those things downtown and take them to her?

It was after three o'clock when Leland finally arrived at the old house beyond the cemetery, the site of Noah Hooper's fox farm before he moved it off the neck. It was isolated from the rest of the village, but had been the only house Ormy could find to rent. Margaret was there to greet him, obviously glad to see someone, even a fourteen-year-old boy. Leland put the groceries on the kitchen table and talked for a few minutes, then excused himself to start working.

The ax, saw and wheelbarrow were in the shed behind the house along with a small pile of firewood. It was a good thing he agreed to cut more. This pile wouldn't last long with the cold weather of October arriving soon. The wood-cutting did not go well. Everything Leland touched was still wet, and he was wet soon after starting. The ax was dull. He could not find a sharpening stone, and the rusty file he did find was not well suited for putting an edge on the ax. The bow saw had a curious tendency to cut in a curve, which made it difficult to work limbs more than a few inches in diameter. Over the next two hours the wood pile doubled in size, although it was made up of pieces from smaller limbs. Leland would bring a good saw and sharpening stone from home next time.

It was turning colder, and Leland's clothes were damp, so after putting the tools away he went back to the house hoping to stand by the stove for a bit before walking home. The kitchen was warm, and Margaret was taking a pan of biscuits out of the oven.

"Leland, take that wet jacket off and sit down at the table to warm up. I'll get you a hot cup of tea and you can have a biscuit or two to go with it. And here's some strawberry jam that I made a few months ago. Ormy says it's the best he's ever had, but he probably says that about your mother's jam, too."

Leland acknowledged that he was cold, and, yes, he would like to stay long enough to warm up. The tea and biscuits with jam were delicious, and he liked talking with Margaret. She asked him about school, his friends, and basketball. He talked about those things, and continued to tell her about June, his classmate. "I like her a lot, and she seems to like me." They went on to discuss siblings and Betty, the new baby. When talk started to lag, Margaret suggested a game of cards, which Leland agreed to. Hearts was his game, so hearts it was. Margaret beat him.

As Leland was putting his jacket on, he looked out the window to find that darkness surrounded the house. He should have been home by now. Mother would wonder where he was and would no doubt tell him of her worries when he got there. The way home was along a gravel road through Danforth's field with a left turn out to Court Street, another half-mile of walking, and finally up State Street. There were no lights until the intersection of Court and State, so it was dark most of the way. An alternate route would be to take a shortcut through the cemetery. It was no darker than going the long way via the streets, and would take less time. When Leland got to the turn in the gravel road that led to Court Street, he chose to go straight ahead across the field, taking advantage of the shortcut.

A partial moon suspended in a now-clear sky allowed him to see the way reasonably well. He hesitated on reaching the iron pipe fence that separated the field from the cemetery. The same moon that lit his way also lit up the gravestones, some showing stark white against the darkness. Shadows from bare tree limbs lay on the ground, moving eerily as the night breeze blew through the cemetery. Maybe it was better to take the long way around. No, he was already late, so he climbed over the fence and made his way among the stones, avoiding areas of tree shadows. There might be something there that would grab his ankles. He took the grassy path that led up the hill. Just before reaching the flagpole at the top, he heard a low moaning sound. He stopped, looked around. Where was it coming from? Above his head. It must be just wind in the tree branches. But it didn't really sound like wind. He stood there looking for something, but what? There seemed to be no movement among the gravestones other than shadows of branches, and now the sound was gone. The wind had died down, too. It must have been wind in the trees. Another gust arrived, stronger than before, and the moan took on a higher pitch. Yes, it was just the wind. He relaxed a bit and started to walk, but continued to look over his shoulder, hoping nothing was after him. As he went past the flagpole a strong gust swept by and a loud snapping noise sounded, like that of a whip. That was one sound too many. Leland took off running as fast as he could. He could think of no reason to spend more time in the cemetery tonight. He approached the fence at high speed, stretched out one hand toward the top rail and vaulted over. He landed in a heap on the other side, but was unhurt, so picked himself up, brushed grass and leaves off his clothes and took one look back. The dim moonlight showed a flag atop the pole flapping furiously in the wind, snapping at times. Leland smiled nervously, then turned to make his way across Alva's cow pasture toward home.

A North Christmas

It was late afternoon on December 22, 1949, in Springport, the last day of school before Christmas break, and Robbie Ellison was walking home from eighth grade basketball practice with Fred and Joel. Wind swept down Ellison Point Road, swirling the last oak leaves and cutting through Robbie's corduroy jacket. He wore a wool sweater under the coat, but was still cold, and it was nearly a mile to his home at the edge of town. Fred and Joel, on the other hand, wore winter coats and were warm enough that they didn't even have them buttoned up all the way. Their talk was about the anticipation of nearly two weeks of no school, no homework, and Christmas presents. The brothers were both hoping for electric train sets, Lionel, not American Flyer, along with model buildings, cars, and people so they could make a railroad town on a sheet of plywood in the basement. Joel looked at Robbie.

"Wha'd you ask for, Robbie? Electric train, too?"

Robbie paused, embarrassed and not knowing how to answer. There was no way that his family could afford a train set.

Last Christmas he had gotten a sweater and two pairs of socks knitted by his mother, a jackknife and a jigsaw puzzle. His nine-year-old sister, Emma, had gotten the same things, except a doll instead of the knife.

He replied, "Naw, I don't really want a train set, and we don't ask for presents anyway, they're supposed to be surprises, so I'll just wait and see what happens. Besides, we're goin' away for Christmas. Visitin' someone in Castine. Be gone for two days."

"Who do you know in Castine? You got relatives there?"

"Nope, it's a friend of my parents, a woman doctor. She lives in a big house down near Dyce's Head. There's goin' to be some other people there, too, from England, I think."

Fred and Joel were both impressed. They had never heard of a doctor who was a woman, and it sounded like she must be rich. Neither of the brothers understood how the Ellisons would get an invitation to a rich doctor's house. Robbie's father, Bob, made a hardscrabble living by digging clams, mowing lawns and doing odd jobs for summer people. His wife, Elissa, tended their large vegetable garden, cleaned houses, and made crabmeat pies that were sold in Taylor's General Store. So, how did they get invited to Castine? Neither knew how to bring that question up; besides, they had reached their house, so just reminded Robbie about playing basketball the next afternoon. They bounded up the front steps, and went in for the usual after-school treat of cookies and milk. Robbie hurried down the road toward home, swinging his arms vigorously in an attempt to keep warm.

The following day was filled with work for each member of the Ellison family. Low tide was at noon, and Dad left home that morning at about nine in his green '38 Ford pickup truck to dig clams. The day before he had cut several oak logs into stove-length pieces, and he got Robbie started on splitting them into stove-size pieces before leaving. Mother worked in the kitchen making food gifts for Dr. North. Truth was that neither she nor Bob knew the doctor, and didn't know why they had been invited to spend Christmas there. The invitation had come through Reverend Harvey, their minister, and perhaps he was responsible. He and Bob worked together on the local Boy Scout troop, and Elissa was a tireless worker in the church women's group. The Ellisons had at first said no, but the good reverend had been persistent in his urging them to accept, and they finally agreed. It was going to be something of an adventure. This morning Elissa and Emma were busy making sugar cookies with sprinkles on top and a loaf of cranberry-nut bread. Emma had picked the cranberries last fall in the bog behind their house.

Robbie finished his wood splitting chores by noon and, after a lunch of a peanut butter sandwich and a still-warm cookie, ran up Ellison Point Road to the school gym to join friends for a game of basketball. They had to wait for the high school students to finish their practice, but played for about an hour before the janitor closed the building.

On the morning of Christmas Eve Robbie helped his dad stack firewood, while Mother and Emma were once again in the kitchen making an apple pie and a crabmeat pie to take to the North house. Robbie could hear them talking and laughing as they worked. Bob left later in the morning to dig clams, promising to be home by three, giving time to get ready for the trip to Castine. Robbie and Emma then helped their mother clean house and after lunch wrapped Christmas presents. Robbie had purchased all of his gifts at the church Christmas fair: a glass candy dish with flowers painted on it for Mother, a book on wild mushrooms for Dad who wanted to learn how to gather edible varieties, a silver bracelet for Emma, and a 1950 calendar with a picture of ducks swimming on a mountain lake with snow-covered peaks in the background for Grampa and Nana Ellison. The grandparents lived at the end of Ellison Point Road, and the younger family would go there for dinner and presents on the day after they returned from Castine.

At three thirty the family members were dressed in their Sunday clothes and in the pickup truck (the Green Jellybean, Dad called it) on the way to Castine. Dad was driving, Mother was on the passenger side with Emma in her lap, and Robbie was in the middle holding a cardboard box that contained the food gifts. One suitcase that held all of their overnight needs was tied down in the back of the truck. They arrived in Castine an hour later, turned right onto Battle Avenue, and went nearly to the end, skirting the main part of town. Dad then turned onto Perkins Street, and at the bottom of the hill made a right onto the gravel driveway that led to a large white house with red trim. It was completely outlined in colored Christmas lights. There were hundreds of lights, but the one thing missing for the Christmas house was snow. The landscape was a dreary mix of gray and brown. The house sat at the edge of an embankment over the Bagaduce River and in the twilight of this winter day gave the family a fine view of the river and Penobscot Bay.

Dad parked Green Jellybean between the two cars already there, both new: one a red Buick convertible, the other a gray Pontiac sedan. Robbie had never been in a house like this and was a bit apprehensive, afraid he would make a fool of himself, but Mother assured him that all would be fine. "Just be yourself, son. You've learned good manners, and you know to be respectful of your elders. Everybody there is going to like you."

Dad, carrying the suitcase, rang the doorbell. It was answered by a middle-aged man, slightly on the heavy side, wearing gray trousers, a white shirt with a green tie and a dark red sweater.

Dr. North's home. Photo courtesy of Wilson Museum

He had a round smiling face that was tanned with the look of one who works outside.

"You must be the Ellisons. Welcome to Dr North's home; we are so glad you can join us. I'm Leon Perkins, and when you need something, just let me know. I'll take care of it."

His appearance and rich bass voice made Robbie like him immediately, and most of his apprehension drained away.

Leon shook hands with each family member and asked their names as they entered the house. He took their coats to hang in a closet near the front door. Robbie was intrigued that Leon had the large calloused hands of a laborer but also the social graces that he observed in summer people. He was at ease with himself and with those around him.

"There are two bedrooms at the top of the stairs that are yours for the night, and your bathroom is in between." Leon took the suitcase from Dad and led the way up with the family following.

Ten minutes later they were all back downstairs. Robbie barely had time to look around the room when a tall, slender woman with black hair swept in and introduced herself as Alice North. She wore a long black skirt, and a white blouse with red vest over it, and had a red rose in her graying hair. She had a no-nonsense look about her. Again, introductions were made, and Mother, who was holding the box of food gifts, said she had some things to contribute for dinner. The two women and Emma disappeared into the kitchen, and Leon excused himself, saying he would be right back but please find a comfortable chair.

Robbie and Dad were left to look around their new surroundings. Dad said the room looked like one in many of the summer "cottages" in Springport, but apparently the house had been winterized. It was warm inside and there were no drafts from the cold wind. A cheerful fire filled a stone fireplace at the far end of the room, and a large fir tree stood in an opposite corner. It was decorated with tinsel, glass balls, popcorn strings and colored lights. Many wrapped packages were tucked under it. Two couches near the fireplace faced each other with a low table between, and two easy chairs were placed near the end of the table away from the fire. Brightly colored rugs covered the floor, paintings were on two walls, and a bookcase nearly filled with volumes covered another. An old drop-leaf table made of pine and showing the patina of age sat under one of the south-facing windows. A large ship model rested on top, its base having a brass plaque with the words "Red Jacket" engraved on it. Robbie noticed a short piece of oak board hanging on the wall beside the fireplace, varnished and mounted in a picture frame without glass. A screwdriver was attached to the oak, not just an ordinary one, rather a Yankee screwdriver. He knew about these, as Grampa Ellison had one in his tool box and prized it highly, but Robbie thought it to be a strange wall decoration.

At about the time they finished their inspection, Leon returned with two other men. The older, a tall slim man with white hair and mustache, was introduced as Major Wright. The other, Lieutenant Grant, was also slim but not as tall, walked with a severe limp, carried a cane and had a nasty scar on his right cheek. Both spoke with accents that Robbie recognized from a movie he had seen last summer. They were English.

The four men moved to the end of the room and stood talking in front of the fireplace. Robbie stayed by a large window looking out at gathering darkness on the river and bay, not knowing what to do, but very soon Lieutenant Grant joined him. He asked where Robbie lived, about his school and what he did for fun. Robbie told him about Springport as being a little town where most families made their living by fishing or working for rich people who owned summer houses there. He said he liked school okay, but mostly liked basketball and spending time with Dad and at his grandparents' house.

Lieutenant Grant said his first name was Albert, but that everyone calls him Grant. "I was named after my pop, and he was named after Prince Albert, but we're not part of the royal family. I grew up in a little village on the southwest coast of England, county of Cornwall. Pop was a fisherman, and I worked with him while growing up. Planned to be a fisherman, too, but was injured during the war, and it ended up that I couldn't do that hard work."

Robbie asked how he had injured his leg, then immediately thought he shouldn't have, but Grant answered.

"I was a pilot in the Royal Air Force. It happened then."

"Oh... What kind of plane did you fly?"

"Learned to fly in a de Havilland Tiger Moth. They were biplanes and built to train pilots. Do you know anything about aeroplanes?"

Robbie nodded, said he liked to read about them, had pictures of lots of different kinds, and liked to build model planes.

"Then you know what a biplane is. Tiger Moths were fun to fly, had two open cockpits, one for the instructor, the other for a trainee. They didn't fly very fast, a little over a hundred miles an hour tops, but they would do all kinds of aero tricks. When you flew upside down, the only thing holding you in was a seat belt. If that failed, you were in trouble. Heard about a chap that had it happen once."

"Wow! Did he have a parachute?"

"No, he didn't. He was in the aft cockpit, and the forward pilot didn't know what had happened, but they were at the top of a loop when he fell, and the plane continued the loop. It got to the bottom at the same time the chap got there, and he landed on top of the fuselage, just aft of his cockpit. He was able to hang on and pull himself forward to crawl back in. The pilot in front of course didn't know anything about it, but two people in a plane nearby saw the whole thing. I was friends with one of those chaps."

Robbie didn't know whether to believe this story on not, it sounded so improbable, but Grant never cracked a smile the whole time, and he showed no indication that it was anything but the truth.

"But, back to my flying. I was assigned to a squadron with Spitfires. Do you know what they are?"

"Yes, I think so. Wasn't it was the main fighter plane used by England? It has kind of oval wings and a glass canopy over the cockpit. Armed with machine guns, and has a big engine. It'll go really fast."

Lt. Grant, formerly of the RAF, was duly impressed that this lad from a small, isolated town in America would know details about Spitfires.

"You're right. They have Rolls Royce Merlin engines, V-12s they are, over a thousand horsepower. When you were sitting at the end of the runway, waiting to take off, and got the word, you pushed the throttle all the way forward. The noise was deafening, and the plane accelerated. You were pushed back into the seat, could hardly move. It was like no acceleration you'll ever have in an automobile. They have a top speed of 350 miles an hour in level flight, and I once got to almost 400 in a dive. It was a real thrill to fly a Spitfire."

"Was your accident in a plane or something else?"

Grant hesitated, not entirely comfortable with the question, but was saved by Leon who arrived carrying a tray with two filled glasses. He passed the larger one to Robbie saying, "This is root beer, hope you like that."

Robbie nodded, took the glass, and said "thank you." Grant reached for the other, a short stout glass with an amber liquid and ice cubes, and sent a grateful look toward Leon. He took a sip of the liquid, closed his eyes, held it in his mouth for a few seconds, then swallowed.

"Cheers, Robbie, and, yes, it was a flying accident. Not really an accident; it went like this. Our group went up to intercept some German bombers that were headed toward London, but of course there were some fighter planes there to protect them. We had a pretty good battle going—we shot down two of their bombers and one fighter. Then the engine on my plane took a hit and started to go down. We were out over the North Sea, and I was able to glide back toward land, but didn't quite make it all the way, so crash landed in the water. My face got cut up, both my legs were broken, and there were a few other problems, but I got out of the plane before it sank. Some local fishermen picked me out of the water. I nearly died, but they got me to a hospital. Ended up staying there for a month. One of my legs was really mangled. You probably noticed it still doesn't work very good."

Grant paused for another sip, thinking that he seldom

talked about this, but somehow this boy was the right audience. He continued.

"After they let me out I couldn't fly any more or do much of anything for that matter. I was really discouraged, just felt sorry for myself. That was when I got an invitation to come over here to spend time at Dr. North's. She brought groups of wounded Brits over on regular basis to recuperate. There were six in my group, and we spent three weeks here. She treated us like kings, and it was the best thing in the world for me. When I got home, felt a hundred percent better, and I got back to living a normal life; found my job at the bank. I'd do anything for that lady—she is one special person. But that's enough about me, I want to hear about you and your family. What does your dad do?"

Robbie had to think about the answer to that question.

"He doesn't have a regular job. In the summer he works for people who come here from Boston and Connecticut. They have summer cottages and are on vacation the whole time here, so don't wanna to work on their houses. They hire Dad to mow lawns, tend gardens, paint and do carpenter jobs. He even fixes their cars sometimes. But what he really likes to do is dig clams. He can dig two bushels in a tide and if the times are right, can get two tides in one day. Sometimes he takes me with him, and it's wonderful to be out there by ourselves, doesn't matter what the weather is. If it's warm and sunny we take our shirts off and feel the sun beat on our backs. It's really peaceful then. If it's cold and rainy it's still nice. The wind usually comes out of the east, right off the water, and it's kind of exciting. The cold isn't a problem because we stay warm by workin' hard. Dad does that year-round, but sometimes in winter the flats freeze up so he can't get to 'em, and there's not as many people around who wanna to buy 'em in the winter. Local people dig their own. Summer people buy 'em."

Encouraged by Grant's apparent interest, Robbie was ready to tell about the rest of his family: mother, sister and grandparents, when Leon returned from the kitchen and announced that dinner was ready. Everyone should go to the table to find their places. He led the way through the door that Robbie had thought led to the kitchen, but was in fact the dining room, the kitchen being the room beyond. The windows here on the south side would provide a view of the bay, except that daylight was now gone, and the only thing visible was a half moon and its reflection on the bay. A large dining table covered with a white cloth was set with silverware and china dishes for eight people. A bouquet of red roses mixed with green cedar branches rested in the middle of the table, flanked by two white flaming candles, each the size of an oatmeal box. The wicks had burned some of the wax to make a crater, and the result was that only the flame tops were directly visible, while most of their light shone through the sides. This was what Mother would call "elegant" and far different than their usual dining space at home where the small maple table from the Grange rummage sale sat in a corner of the kitchen. It usually had a red and white checkered cloth that covered stains and scratches on the tabletop, and was big enough for four people, six in a squeeze. But now Robbie realized that each plate on this table held a small card with a name written on it, and he was to find the one with his name. After several minutes of shuffling, everyone was in place, standing behind a chair, Dr. North at one end of the table, Leon at the other end near the kitchen door. Robbie was in the middle of one side between Major Wright and Emma and directly across from Mother. He wondered if she had arranged to be there so she could kick his ankle if needed. Major Wright stepped over to Dr. North's chair, pulled it back. then edged it in as she sat. This was the sign for everyone to sit except for Leon who moved around the table with a tray and set a small glass dish filled with fruit salad on each plate. When he had finished and taken his place, Dr. North asked Major Wright to say grace.

"Dear Heavenly Father, we thank you for this day, the celebration of your gift to us, your Son, who has shown us the light and redeemed our souls. We thank you also for this dear lady who has helped us in our time of need. We are grateful for this Christmas feast and ask that others may fare as well as we. Finally, we pray that lasting peace may finally come to this troubled world. Amen."

Several "amens" followed, and Christmas diner began. The fruit dish was followed by cups of lobster stew and warm slices of crusty bread. Then Leon brought in a huge roast beef and dishes of mashed potatoes, gravy, carrots and peas. The latter must have been the frozen kind as they were slightly crunchy and bright green, not the mushy pale-green peas that came from a can. There was also something called Yorkshire pudding, which Major Wright said must always be served with roast beef.

Emma whispered to Robbie, "It doesn't taste like pudding, it's more like scrambled eggs, but pretty good. I helped cook it, and we baked it in the oven in the roast beef pan after the roast came out. Mother knows how to make it now, and we'll have it at home."

Robbie was willing to try new foods, and liked most, so Yorkshire pudding was easy. It, along with the rest of the meal, was absolutely delicious. The dish of brown sticky condiment that came his way, called chutney, was something of a stretch, but Major Wright said it was good, and so it was.

The meal continued in relative silence for some time with only an occasional exclamation about one of the dishes served, but as appetites became satiated, conversation picked up. Dr. North related that the two English guests had arrived in Castine the previous week after eight days of travel by ship from Southampton, England, to New York, and the train trip to Bangor. She said, "Major Wright, I recall that you and I have a common interest in carpentry tools. Is that right?"

"It is, indeed, and one of my prized possessions is a Yankee screwdriver, model 2800, that you gave me in 1944 when I was your guest here in this house. For those who don't know, Dr. North's father, along with his two brothers, founded the North Brothers Manufacturing Company, and their most famous product was the Yankee screwdriver. Now, Dr. North, you said we have a common interest in carpentry tools. I think your interest lies in the fact that your family company manufactured them, and my interest is that my family company sells them. If any of you are in Bristol and looking for tools or a variety of other things, look us up. We're called Wright Brothers, Ironmongers."

There were puzzled expressions around the table. Leon said, "Ironmongers?"

"Yes. Oh... I guess that's not a word that's used here very much, but it means the same thing as what you might call a hardware store. And we do sell Yankee screwdrivers there, although they are now made by Stanley Tools."

Dr. North interrupted. "Stanley bought out North Brothers in 1938. Marketing just a few products became difficult, and Stanley has a wide range of tools along with a marketing system and factories both here and in England. It made sense for our line of tools to merge with them."

Elissa Ellison asked, "What is a Yankee screwdriver?"

Bob immediately replied, "You know what they are. It's the kind that you push on the handle to turn the screw instead of turning the whole screwdriver. Dad has a couple of 'em."

"Oh, I know what you're talkin' about."

"They're much easier to use than a regular screwdriver, and

Dad especially likes them, what with arthritis in his hands. But I didn't know there was a Maine connection with the North family," Bob said, looking at Dr. North.

"There's more than just a family connection to Maine. The idea was invented and patented by a Maine man, Zachary Furbish. I think he lived somewhere over in the western part of the state, maybe around Rumford. My uncle read of his invention in a newspaper article and contacted him about a partnership. Zachary was smart as a whip, but didn't have any money to develop his ideas, so my uncle bought the patent rights and also hired him to work for North Brothers. But that's enough about screwdrivers. Mrs. Ellison, I could tell after just a few minutes of your being in my kitchen that you know a lot about cooking. Do you do that as a business?"

Elissa, who had been at first shy, was now encouraged by the interest shown from this woman at the end of the table. She told about making crabmeat pies for sale and organizing many of the church suppers that were held throughout the year. She also related, with some pride, that she had recently been hired to cater the dinners that were held weekly during July and August at the Springport Golf Club. The conversation then moved on to others telling about their lives. Leon told of boyhood adventures on the farm in Penobscot that had been in his family since 1770 and which he still owned. He and his brothers helped with farm chores and learned to hunt and fish. Bob told about their family home in Springport and his efforts at a variety of jobs. Lt. Grant explained that his home town was, in many ways, similar to the coastal towns in this part of Maine, and that he came from a fishing family. Major Wright's schoolboy years were spent at Eton, and as an adult, except for the war, he had worked in the family business. Even shy Emma related her love of reading and how she wanted to be a teacher. Elissa noticed that, like Bob, neither Major Wright nor Lt. Grant spoke about their wartime experiences.

After more than an hour of conversation and eating, Leon rose and went to the kitchen, apparently intent on preparing the next course. Robbie joined his mother and Emma in clearing the table and bringing dessert plates, cups and saucers and a huge pot of tea from the kitchen. When all except Leon were again seated, he emerged carrying a platter that contained a brown mass that vaguely resembled a football and was completely engulfed by flames. Major Wright let out a cheer, and shouted, “Well done, my good man, well done!”

Leon beamed as he placed the platter in front the Major, and said, “This is an English plum cake, a joint effort of the Major and me. He provided the recipe and some special ingredients, then supervised the preparation. I just carried out his orders. It was supposed to age for a month or two, but we only made it a few days ago. Hopefully the flaming brandy will make up for it being fresh.”

Major Wright cut the cake and spooned a white frosting-like sauce over each piece while Dr. North poured tea. Servings were passed around the table. Robbie noticed that Emma was looking at her dessert with a mix of question and panic. It looked a bit like the fruit cake that grandmother Ellison made, and Emma had never been a fan of that. Robbie nudged her elbow, caught her eye and gave a vigorous nod. She understood that to mean she should eat the cake, which turned out to be very good. Robbie wondered if Mother were upset over her children eating brandy-soaked cake, but she seemed absorbed in enjoying her own dessert.

After dinner Bob volunteered that he and Robbie would wash dishes. Leon insisted that he be part of the process so that dishes would end up in their proper places. Everyone else moved to the living room and found seats near the fire that Leon had tended several times during dinner. Emma snuggled up close to her mother on a couch and decided that this was the best Christmas Eve ever. Bob and Robbie finally finished their work in the kitchen, but as they left to join the others, Leon was busy with more food preparations: Mother's cranberry bread and sugar cookies on plates, fruit punch poured into a large bowl, and two gallons of apple cider with cinnamon added set on the stove to heat. Robbie had no idea why all of this was happening. Leon was fixing enough food and drink for dozens of hungry people, and there were no hungry people in this house.

When they returned to the living room, others were recounting how they celebrated Christmas. There were surprisingly few differences between Christmas at the Ellisons' in Maine, the North family in Philadelphia, and the visitors in western England. All included good things to eat, special church services, carol-singing, Christmas trees, Santa Claus, and presents for loved ones. It occurred to Robbie that this evening had included some of those: special food, Christmas tree with presents, and Dr. North had mentioned a Christmas Eve church service for later in the evening. No doubt Mother would see to it that the Ellison family went to that. But there had been no carol singing, and that was always part of the Ellison house Christmas Eve. Just at that moment the headlights of several cars shone in the driveway. They were shining through swirling snow flakes. There would be snow for Christmas!

Leon had seen the lights, too, went to the front door, and, opening it, called out, "Merry Christmas, come in out of the snow! We hoped you would come."

Soon fifteen or twenty people had crowded through the front door, stamping snow from boots and removing coats, hats, scarves and mittens. It was a grand mix of children, teenagers, young adults and a few "old people." Dr. North was in their midst, greeting them, calling many by name, and finally conferring with

Mr. Pratt, who seemed to be in charge of the group. He herded them into a semicircle around the room facing the fireplace and the North House guests, then directed them in singing "Silent Night." Next came "God Rest Ye Merry Gentlemen" and Mr. Pratt urged everyone to join in. Several more familiar carols followed, and Robbie noticed that, like the Ellisons, Major Wright and Lt. Grant knew the words. The group finished by singing "We Wish You a Merry Christmas," then everyone gathered around the table where Leon had set out food and drinks. Conversation and laughter continued for some time, but by nine fifteen the singers had left, and relative quiet settled into the North House.

The quiet did not last. Robbie, sitting on a couch next to Dad, feeling the warmth from the fire, and hearing the low hum of several conversations, was close to falling asleep when the loud announcement was made: "Time to go to church." So everyone roused, put on coats and boots and headed out the door. Leon and Dr. North drove their cars, with Robbie and Emma in the front seat of Leon's Pontiac. It had an automatic transmission and a radio.

The service was in the Episcopal Chapel, a stone building on Perkins Street not far from Dr. North's house. During the service Robbie was mostly lost about what to say and do, and noted with satisfaction that Mom, Dad, Emma, and even Leon had the same problem. But there was a familiar Bible reading about the birth of Jesus, and they sang familiar carols. At the end of the service, several people greeted the Ellisons and wished them a merry Christmas. It was nearly eleven when they returned to the North House, and after Leon had set cookies and milk on the table by the fireplace, everyone went to bed.

Robbie snuggled into his bed under a warm comforter and was nearly asleep when Emma whispered, "Robbie, are you awake?"

"Yep."

"I didn't wanna come here for Christmas, but it's been pretty nice, don't you think?"

"Yeah, it's been fun. I like Lt. Grant and Leon—well, everyone really, and it was fun having the carolers come. Leon said they went to lots of other houses first, but just stayed outside to sing. They came here last."

"Do you think we could tell Mr. Harvey about it, and maybe next year our church group could do it? I'd like to go around town singing carols."

"We can try. Go to sleep now."

"I can't sleep, there's a hundred things goin' around in my head."

"You've got to go to sleep. Santa won't stop here if he knows you're awake."

"I don't think there's any Santa Claus. I think Mom and Dad put presents under the tree."

Outside their window the jingle of sleigh bells was heard along with huffing noises that sounded vaguely like horses... or reindeer.

"What was that?"

"It was probably Santa, but I don't know if he'll stop here after what you just said."

"Ya think so?"

"G' night, Emma."

"Merry Christmas, Robbie."

The last thing Robbie heard before sleep was the downstairs front door opening, then closing.

Christmas morning at the North house came early for the Ellison children. They woke up at four o'clock, but didn't dare to go downstairs so talked for a while, then fell asleep again. The next thing they heard was Leon was calling up the stairs.

"Robbie and Emma! Santa must have come last night. You need to come down here and see what he left."

They dressed and hurried down the stairs to find the adults already up and sitting by the fire drinking steaming mugs of spiced cider left over from last night. They also saw two large felt stockings with their names embroidered on them, hanging from hooks at the side of the fireplace. With a little encouragement from Dr. North, the children took the stockings from the hooks and peered inside. Robbie's held an orange, an Almond Joy candy bar, a pair of leather mittens, and a balsa wood model airplane kit—Piper Cub version with tissue paper for fuselage covering and rubber band-powered propeller. It had a twenty-four inch wingspan. Emma's stocking had similar contents except there was a leather-bound writing journal and a purple fountain pen instead of the airplane kit.

Everyone then went to the dining room for a breakfast of sausage and pancakes with maple syrup prepared by Leon, and a fruit salad by Elissa. Robbie was surprised to see that the two English guests had tea instead of coffee. With breakfast finished and dishes stacked in the kitchen, the group moved back to the living room and gathered around the tree. Dr. North asked Leon to act as Santa Claus, and he agreed, reading names on tags and handing presents to those named. The children received more than what seemed like their fair share, but no one objected.

The Ellisons' afternoon packing process was considerably more complicated than when they had left Springport, as many of the presents under the tree had been for them. Each family member had a new winter coat. Mother received the recent edition of *Joy of Cooking* and Dad now had his own Yankee screwdriver. Emma had several new outfits to wear and books: Nancy Drew mysteries, *The Wizard of Oz*, a dictionary, and three volumes of poetry. Robbie had been given an American Flyer train set, a circus train version, and three volumes of The Hardy Boys mystery books.

By mid-afternoon the Ellisons were ready to start for home. There were hugs and handshakes all around. Robbie was glad to get handshakes. During the drive back to Springport there was steady conversation about the past twenty-four hours. All enthused about the presents they received, but Mother said that the best part was the time spent with those four lovely people. Robbie thought about that and decided maybe it was true, but he really liked his train set.

Obadiah

My name is Obadiah, and I'm a dog. Yes, I know, most dogs don't talk, at least not when people are around, but I've learned to communicate with some and don't see any reason not to use that skill. You seem to be one who does understand me, so if you're willing to spend some time, I'll tell you a bit about myself and about my town, Castine. It's not a very big town, but I like it and think you will, too. First, something about me.

I was born in 1941 on a farm in New Hampshire, so I'm not a native Mainer. Hope you won't hold that against me, although I understand that some have biased views about that sort of thing. I've overheard my people talk about my mother as being a large Newfoundland bitch. No, that's not a bad word. She had unusual coloring for her breed, black and white like me. I was one of six pups resulting from a night of passion that she shared with a neighboring hound dog. That makes me an illegitimate child, but that's normal for dogs. Again, I hope that doesn't bother you. My original family had their milk delivered by a neighboring dairy farmer, and at about two months of age, I was traded to that farmer for a week's delivery of milk, ten quarts I believe. Soon after that a big war started, and the farmer was invited to rejoin the Navy. He had done that twenty-five years previously for another big war, but he accepted the invitation anyway, leaving his wife and children to tend the cows, an apple orchard and a barn full of chickens. This situation was not popular with the family, so the farm was sold and they moved to a city. When the war ended there was no farm to go back to and no one liked the city, so they moved here, to Castine.

This big old house behind us is where I live now, at the corner of Court and Green streets. Across Court Street is the town common; that's the library to the left, the grammar school is at the top of the hill, the high school is over in that other corner, and at the bottom of that hill is the Unitarian church. There are lots of people coming and going most of the time, so my yard is a good place to keep track of what's happening in this part of town.

I take long walks every day, sometimes with one of my family, sometimes by myself. I've gotten to know most of the dogs and people who live in the neighborhood. I get along well with most of the dogs, even play with a few. There are two bitches that I'm especially fond of, and there have been a number of puppies born who look remarkably like me. There are several dogs with personality defects, and whenever the chance happens along I give them a thrashing. Skippy Perkins, a mean-spirited little terrier who bites people for no reason, is the worst of them. I thoroughly enjoy thrashing him.

I'm more of a people-dog than a dog-dog. I enjoy people's company and have found that most are good-hearted and friendly. There are many who, when I meet them, will say, "Hello, Obadiah," and a few will even stop to talk. The conversation is usually limited as most have difficulty understanding me, but if I wag my tail and look them in the eye they seem satisfied and continue on their way in a better mood than before we met. I like to think that a town dog's job is to make people happy, make them smile. In spite of my best efforts, however, there are a few who completely ignore me. If they have a scowl when we meet, they continue to scowl after we pass. That's a shame. Then there are a very few who just don't like dogs. Maybe they had a bad experience with one antisocial dog and now hold that experience against all of us. It seems quite unfair to be put on a list of undesirables without having earned that distinction, but I understand there are groups of people subject to that same attitude from some of their fellow humans. It seems to me that disliking someone you don't know and know nothing about is a poor way to spend your life. There must be better activities to occupy the time we have here. But enough of classifying people and dogs. Let's take a walk to introduce you to this neighborhood, 1947 version.

Obadiah gets a hug. Photo courtesy of Mary Danforth Lozier

I live with my people: two boys ages 9 (Donald) and 18 (David) and their parents, Harry and Helen. There are two older girls, Mary and Sylvia, but they're adults and live out of state. Harry teaches at Maine Maritime Academy, and Helen runs the house. Right now they're negotiating with Clarence Wheeler to buy the Castine Coal Company, and if that happens, Helen will run that. Keep the books, that is, not deliver the coal. Lossie Littlefield does that. Harry says he doesn't understand how a family can live on twenty dollars a week, so plans to increase Lossie's pay to twenty-five dollars.

The house is one hundred fifty years old and needs a lot of repair work. Alva Clement and his crew are doing that now. The sills in the main house are being replaced, and the red barn at the back is being torn down. When the barn was built everyone had horses and probably a cow or two, but we don't have those big animals now, only a small flock of chickens in a hen house in the back yard. When those two jobs are finished, the crew will go on to removing the top floor of the ell. That part of the house was built about a hundred years ago. It has two kitchens on the first floor and lots of tiny bedrooms on the second. They used to be rented to rusticators in the summer and Normal School students in the winter, but the Normal School is closed and rusticators want more elegant accommodations.

You may have noticed that elderly woman in a long black dress sitting on the library steps. That's Alice Gardner. She's not supposed to be out by herself, but she wanders off sometimes. She and her sister, Cad Carter, live in the house by the grammar school. There's a rumor that they have lots of money—big old fashioned bills hidden around the house—but they don't live like rich people. She's sitting there because she's tired after walking downtown and back, so is just resting before that final walk up the hill. If I go over to see her, she'll give me an Oreo cookie. They're not good for me, but they taste good. Oh, and that's George Richardson coming down the hill. He's the janitor at the grammar school. His brother, Chuckie, or Charles, is Postmaster, and he has a twin brother, Frank. George and Frank are ushers at the Main Street Church every Sunday.

Looking down Green Street, the first house on the left is where the Bowdens live. There are lots of Bowdens in Castine, but that is the Lester Bowden family. Lester works for the water company. He drives around in a pickup truck, and when he sees a child or dog he scares us by swerving the truck in our direction and revving the engine. I don't think he's a bad person, just greets us that way. When Lester talks he ends almost every sentence with "See?" I don't know why. Lester's son, Delly, lives there, too, and works on trees: planting, trimming, pruning, things like that. He is going to plant cedar trees to make a hedge around two sides of our property. Mother says he drinks beer, but I think that's okay. Sometimes in the late afternoon when I'm lying quietly in the yard, I can hear him playing guitar and singing. The songs are about Castine, and he makes them up. His most famous one is "On Saturday Night The Boodens Come To Town." Father told him that they're good, and he should write them down so they don't get lost, but Delly doesn't read or write music. I suppose they will get lost. Oh, and Delly used to be a prizefighter, too. Lester's other son, Hazelton, lives with his family in the yellow house farther down the street. He was in the war, but is now a cabinet maker and has a shop in the little building next to the house. He's planning to go to Farmington Normal School and learn to be a shop teacher.

Percy Wardwell lives in one of the houses between Lester and Hazelton. His wife is from Old Town, a Penobscot Indian. They both seem nice enough, but I can't get them to pay any attention to me. John and Doris Pratt and their son Jay live in the house below Hazelton. John is a salesman for Timken oil burners, and Doris is part of the Wardwell family. There are lots of Wardwells in town. Gus and Algie Wardwell live across the street from them, and have a grocery store downtown. If you stay here for long, you'll need to go into Wardwell's Sanitary Market. Coming back up the hill, George and Edith Coombs live in this end of the big house. George runs the hardware store, and Edith is the town clerk, plus she works in the library sometimes. The bungalow across the street from Lester is the Robinsons' house. They own the drugstore, and both work there. Directly across Green Street from here is the home of Joe and Prue Devereux. He's a yacht captain, and his boss likes to have the boat available year-round, so Joe isn't home very often.

Let's start walking east along Court Street. Oh, it's called that because Castine used to be the Hancock County seat, and the county courthouse was right there where the library is now. The house that's down this driveway to the right used to be the Methodist parsonage, and the church used to be between the street and the house. It's obviously gone now, but those granite blocks arranged in a rectangle were the foundation stones for the church. The Wilbert Gray family lives there now. Most people call him Winkey. He has three brothers: Cooler, Nutty, and James. I don't know where James got his name. Winky's daughter Bunny is Don's age, and son Richard is Dave's age. Winkey does yard work in the summer, traps fur animals in the winter, and hunts all year. They also raise pigs, and at butchering time you can hear the pigs squealing blocks away. The next house, with a picket fence, is where the Mayos live. Bud Mayo keeps bees in his back yard and runs the IGA grocery store downtown. The Unitarian Church, on that side of the street, is another very old building. Paul Revere made the bell that hangs in the tower. Next to the church is George Faye's house. He has the only taxi business in town, and runs it out of that garage next to the house. No, I'm wrong. Joe Dennett will taxi people too, but he's mostly busy with the boat business at Dennett's Wharf that he runs with his brother, Jake. Joe knows a lot about cars and engines because he was an ambulance driver and mechanic in World War I. Joe does all of the engine and electrical work at the wharf, while Jake builds and repairs boats. That big white house coming up next, the one that looks like mine, is the Hale house. The Hale family has lived there since it was built nearly one hundred fifty years ago. Jimmy Hale has two cows and a big flock of chickens. Everyone in the Hale family is deaf, and they talk with each other using their hands. The problem is, almost no one else in town understands that, so they carry little notebooks and pencils to communicate. Strange thing is, Jimmy and I understand each other perfectly.

The building beyond George Faye's garage is the Castine Hospital. Dr. Babcock runs it, or at least he takes care of people there. I think that Beulah Rowell, the head nurse, is the one who actually runs the hospital. Dr. Harold Babcock is a wonderful man, but he works too hard. He spends all day at the hospital and making house calls, and then may be up all night delivering a baby. That might be here or it might be at someone's house maybe in Bucksport or Deer Isle. When he's not doing doctor work he likes to fish and bird hunt. He has a bird dog I'm acquainted with, but they don't go hunting often enough. The doctor also likes to play poker, and there's a group that does that quite regularly: Dr. Babcock, Jimmy Hale, Ralph Wardwell, Dr. Pierce, and Spunk Hatch. Spunk and his wife, Laura, named their oldest son Harold Babcock Hatch after the doctor.

The house coming up on the other side of the hospital is where my family used to live before they went to New Hampshire. Mary's and Sylvia's bedroom, on the second floor, faced the hospital and had a fine view of the operating room window. There were no curtains, and the children soon discovered that they could watch all kinds of interesting happenings, like operations and babies being born. One day Beulah looked up and saw them in the window. Curtains were installed the next day. The house beyond that, the old one that looks like it's about to fall in, is the Perkins House, and it was built when this was still a British colony. It's haunted. My family still talks about hearing strange noises coming from the house in the middle of the night. There's a hole in the back wall, and I went in once. Didn't hear any noises, but when I got to the living room a rocking chair started to rock all by itself. I got out of there fast.

The house we're coming to now, on the right, is where the Allens live. George works at the insurance office and always wears a dress shirt and tie, even when he's working in his yard, although he doesn't do that often any more. In fact, there's Coppy Webster right now weeding the flower garden. Coppy has just a few yards that he

The Perkins House at its original Court Street location.

Photo courtesy of Leland Bowden

looks after, but mostly he's downtown sitting on the bench by Bob Bowden's barber shop. He usually knows what's going on in town. Sometimes when I stop to see him he gives me a Fig Newton.

The Danforths live here on the corner of Court and Dyers Lane. They've always been good friends with my family, and I spend a lot of time here with Donald and several other children. Mary Danforth is the leader of that group. They're all boys except for Mary, but she's the boss. Her mother, Ethelyn, teaches at the grammar school, and father, Roger, used to be a teacher, but he now has a chicken farm off the neck. We sometimes get to go with him and play at the farm. George Dunbar and his wife live at the farmhouse. She's English, and they met when George was in the Army, stationed in England. The kids really like her. She tells them about living in England during the war while they have tea and cookies in the afternoon. She also tells jokes, the kind that other adults never tell to kids. They laugh and laugh and try to remember to tell other friends.

You may not know what "off the neck" means. Well, Castine village is almost an island, but it's connected to the mainland by a low, narrow piece of land. The almost-island part of town is sort of like a head, the mainland sort of like a body, and they're connected by "the neck," so the mainland part is "off the neck" from the village.

If you look down Dyers Lane there's a house on the left where Horace and Marie Leach live. Horace owns the Chevrolet garage downtown. Their son Willis was in the war, but he's home now and works at the garage. Willis has a motorcycle. He took the muffler off and rides it around town in the middle of the night. People get some irritated.

This little house on the right is where Mrs. Carter, her son Bobby and her sister live. Bobby's in Donald's class, and he comes to our house sometimes.

Next on Court Street, to the left, is the Clements' house. Alva is a carpenter. That's his shop in one of those two little barns next to the house. He has several men working for him, Woodrow Bakeman for one. He's another boy just back from the war. Alva builds and repairs houses, and is doing the work on my family's house. The cow in that field across the street belongs to them. Alva grew up on a farm in Penobscot, and likes to keep a cow just because he likes cows and doesn't like pasteurized milk. The Clements don't have any children, but they did raise Lorna's nephew, Eddie Douglas. He and his wife Therma live in that house next to the cow pasture. It was Lorna's family home. Therma's family lives just down the hill below the pasture on Water Street. Eddie and Therma are wonderful singers. I heard them sing a duet just last week at the Castine Variety Show in the town hall. I sat out on the lawn and could hear through the windows. They were the best act of the whole night.

Here we are at State Street, and the field on the far corner is another pasture that belongs to Alva. He'll probably cut it for hay this year. Mows by hand with a scythe, then uses a big wooden hand rake, and loads it into the back of his truck with a pitchfork. Stows the hay in the loft of one barn, and the cow lives downstairs in that barn when she's not out in the field. They also keep chickens in a little hen house by their garden. The first house up State Street is where Ormy and Margaret Bowden live. Their daughter, Betty, is in Donald's class, and she comes to our house sometimes. They put on a play a few weeks ago along with Bunny Gray, Bonny Mayo and Keith Perkins. They wrote it and were the actors. Charged five cents admission and made eighty-five cents. Ormy is Therma's brother, but I don't think they're related to Lester. Lester grew up in Hardscrabble; Ormy's family's been here for a long time.

Hardscrabble is a community between here and Bucksport, part in Penobscot, part in Orland, but it's kind of like a separate town. People in Hardscrabble have their own way of talking. I've already told you about Lester saying "See?," but there's more to it than that. They pronounce words different than people in Castine or in other parts of Penobscot and Orland. Some say it's the way words were pronounced in rural England three hundred years ago. Luther Bridges lives in Hardscrabble and mows lawns here in Castine, so I know him. He's Bobby Carter's uncle and a nice man, always speaks to me and has even shared a sandwich, but I have trouble understanding him. I just pretend to understand and wag my tail.

Looking farther up State Street, you can see there are two houses beyond Ormy's. Bert Stover lives in the first one. He has a Ford Model A truck and does lawn work. He's quite old though, so it must be almost time to retire. The house beyond that, the new one, belongs to Ormy's younger brother, Gene. He brings the mail down from Bucksport. If you've got an errand or two to do there, he'll give you a ride up and back for a dollar. Gene also has a hotdog stand down at the town wharf. A hotdog costs fifteen cents, and Donald really likes 'em with fried onions and mustard. He usually shares with me if I sit in front of him and drool. The house across from Bert Stover's is where the McLaughlin family lives. You'll notice that the house sticks out into the sixth fairway of the golf course. Well, last week Father drove a golf ball right through the living room window. No one was home, but he owned up to it later. That's been a problem, so the golf club is going to put a high fence between the house and the tee to catch golf balls before they get to the window.

Back here on Court Street, the big house on the right belongs to the Ushers, but they only live here for a few months in the summer. He's a professor at some famous college, Harvard maybe, and is always too busy thinking to pay any attention to me. The house used to belong to Miss Hathaway, and she wrote a best-selling book, *The Little Locksmith*. Lorna says she wrote it there in that little shed to the left of the house, but someone else claims she wrote it in Blue Hill. Either way, you can read about Lorna in the book.

This is the last house on Court Street, so we'll turn around here, but if we kept going we'd come to Spring Street which has just one house, Captain Ladd's. He owns the mail boat *Hippocampus* that goes from Castine to Islesboro to Belfast and back to Castine six days a week. He takes passengers, too, so if you want to shop in Belfast, just ride over with him. That's how the high school basketball team gets to Islesboro for basketball games, but it's a special trip that leaves late afternoon and doesn't get back until almost midnight.

Spring Street is not very long, and at the bottom of the hill it curves around to the right and becomes Water Street, and has the reputation of being the rough part of town. I guess it used to be. When Castine was a busy seaport that's where sailors came ashore to find excitement. There were bars and lots of entertainment, some of which we're not supposed to talk about. That's all gone now, and the people who live there are hard workers. Walter Farley is a carpenter, Joel Perkins is a painter, Mace Eaton builds boats, and Marie Wood sells dairy farm supplies like milk bottle caps. By the way, Joel Perkins is painting the inside of my family's house, and it's taking a long time. He told someone downtown that Harry Small, on his teacher's salary, will go broke trying to pay him, so he doesn't bother to charge for some of the days he works.

Ed Bridgeham, an old bachelor, lives on Water Street, too. He's in the house below the Ushers' and has always kept a cow in the field between the two houses. The other day when I was out checking the neighborhood, I happened to go down through that field. There was Ed digging a big hole. I went over to see what that was about, and found that his cow had died right there in the field that morning. Ed was burying her. I went over to tell him I was sorry, and he got right down on his knees and hugged me. He was crying. I hope he gets another cow. He lives all alone and needs something to give him a purpose in life.

Oh, here we are back at Alva's field, and that's the back of Ida Bowden's house down on Water Street. Ida makes donuts on Thursday—that's today—and they are really good. If I go scratch on her back door she might give me one. I'll leave you here and go try for a donut, but maybe you'd like to explore the rest of the town on your own. It's not very big, so you won't get lost.

Wilburt Remembered

December, 2015: A storm arrived in Castine one day last week, covering brown trees and muddy roads with a pristine white coat. It was the first substantial snowstorm of the year and was greeted with enthusiasm by most. A few grumpy souls complained, but children were excited to have a chance to slide on the golf course sixth fairway just as I did nearly seventy years ago. Owners of pickup trucks with snowplows were happy to have a chance to earn a few dollars plowing neighbors' driveways. Photographers took the opportunity to record the town in its winter finery. Snowmobilers raced around the golf course by moonlight. Cross-country skiers slipped across open fields and under snow-ladened branches while snowshoers made trails in their own plodding way. Shelley and I are in that latter group, so after the driveway was cleared using the snowblower, and the walkways were cleared using shovels, we retrieved our snowshoes from their place at the back of the garage.

Shelley has a pair from L.L. Bean: pink aluminum frames

with sheets of gray plastic stretched across and boot harnesses riveted in the center. I have a similar pair, different colors, that I inherited from Bary. I like them because they were hers. However, they're not big enough to hold my weight in snow more a few inches deep, and walking in a few inches of snow doesn't require snowshoes, so I reached for the other pair made of ash wood and leather and shaped like teardrops. They are light and big enough to support my weight in deep snow. This is "Winkey's pair."

Wilburt "Winkey" Gray and his family were our neighbors during the years around 1950, living in what was originally the Methodist Church parsonage. The house sits well back from Court Street and across from the town common. The space between the house and street was the location of the church; however, that was torn down in the early 1940s. A story from my family concerning the house when it was a parsonage is that my older sister, Mary, was playing with the minister's daughter one day when they decided it would be exciting to take their tricycles to the porch roof, which was nearly level. They had a wonderful time until Mary rode her tricycle off the edge. She landed in the top of a bush near the ground where the tricycle was demolished, but fortunately Mary was not seriously hurt.

The Grays were a large family that included a daughter, Bernice (Bunny) who was in the same class as I at Adams School and later Castine High School. Her older brother, Richard, was in the same class as my brother, David. There was a friendly if not close relationship between the families. As with many in the 1940s, with the Depression barely over and prosperity not yet returned to Maine, the Gray family finances were probably not easy. Winkey worked as a groundskeeper at Maine Maritime Academy during the lawn-mowing and leaf-raking seasons, but the job did not extend into the winter months. They had a large garden in a field behind Adams School. They kept a flock of chickens, a pig was raised every year, and Winkey was a hunter, a very good hunter. He always got a deer during the fall season as did several other household members. A rumor suggested that perhaps venison was served at the Gray house during other seasons as well. And finally, he was a fur trapper. In winter and early spring the back porch of their house was lined with fox pelts hanging from the edge of the roof made famous by Mary and her tricycle.

My father's name was Harrison, but as a child and young adult he was called "Sonny." He thoroughly disliked that name, felt degraded by it and was eventually able to leave it behind except at family gatherings of his siblings and father. So he was sensitive to nicknames that burdened others, and felt that his next door neighbor probably did not like what most people called him, Winkey. He was Wilburt to my father.

One January evening just after a storm had dumped nearly two feet of snow on Castine, Wilburt appeared at our door.

"Is your father home?"

"Yep. Dad, Mr. Gray's here."

Dad, an English teacher, was correcting student essays at the time. He came through from his den at the back of the house, greeted Wilburt, and invited him into the living room.

"I got my snowshoes out this morning, but when I put 'em on, the frame of one broke right in half, and the other doesn't look much better. I've got to tend my traps, but the snow's so deep I can't get to 'em. Have you got a pair of snowshoes I could borrow?"

Dad allowed that he did have a pair, an old pair that was not in very good condition. "They're out in the garage. Let's go look at them, and if you think they'll do, you're welcome to borrow them." Wilburt went home with a sorry-looking pair of snowshoes: weather-beaten frames, missing pieces of leather thong webbing, and makeshift harnesses of rope.

He kept them well beyond the end of trapping season, but I don't think my Dad gave it much thought or even cared if they were returned. One fine spring evening, however, Wilburt showed up at our front door with snowshoes in hand. They bore little resemblance to the pair he had borrowed several months before. The ash-wood frames had been sanded and refinished with varnish, the leather webbing had been completely replaced and a new set of hand-made boot harnesses installed. They were beautiful, and now, nearly seventy years later, they are still a joy to see and touch. The original lettering on the frames is faintly visible:

AROOSTOOK
MANUFACTURED ESPECIALLY FOR
RICE AND MILLER CO.
BANGOR MAINE

The design of these snowshoes evolved over probably thousands of years of use by North American Indians. Now, in the early part of the twenty-first century, this type is still available and made by hand. Although considerably more expensive than the aluminum and plastic version, the joy of ownership is definitely in their favor. The elegant design is a reminder of an ancient heritage, and this particular pair is a reminder of Wilburt Gray and the 1950 version of Castine that he knew.

Duck Hunting with Dad

It was a cold early-December Saturday morning when Dick and his brother were awakened by their father.

"Time to get up, boys, we're going duck huntin' this mornin'. Need to be on the way before sun-up."

Dick peered out from under the quilt and through the east-facing window of the bedroom that he shared with his older brother, Linny. It was still dark, but a thin red layer defined the horizon, predicting that sun-up would soon arrive. He wondered if that red also was a prediction of bad weather. "Red in the morning, sailors take warning" was advice that usually turned out to be accurate. The room was cold, and it would be nice to stay in his warm, comfortable bed, but that was not part of the morning plan. He reached out from under the quilt, retrieved yesterday's pair of wool socks, and pulled them on before getting out of bed. Linny was already up, dressed, and headed for the kitchen. Dick did a quick switch from pajamas to long johns, wool pants, flannel shirt and sweater, plus another pair of socks, then went downstairs for breakfast.

Dad was outside feeding the chickens and would be ready to go very soon, so there was no time for the usual fare of hot cereal followed by bacon and eggs. A quick meal of toast with peanut butter and a glass of milk sufficed. Dick put on his new pair of green rubber boots. His old pair was not worn out, but his eight-year-old body had grown, and last year's boots were too small. They would be passed on to one of his sisters. Linny picked up two guns from a corner in the back hall, a twenty-gauge shotgun and a twenty-two rifle plus ammunition for both. Dick carried the dinner box that Mom had filled with chicken salad sandwiches and a thermos of hot tea, and the boys went outside looking for Father. Spot and Wags, their two hounds, were waiting, tails wagging. They were not duck hunters as they didn't like to swim, but were eager to go whatever the destination. Dad, just returning from the chicken house, trudged through the four-inch layer of wet, heavy snow that had fallen yesterday. The snow hid the brown and gray landscape that often defines early winter.

They left the house via the back door and along the porch where several fox pelts hung. Their father, Wilburt (or Winky as he was commonly known), mowed lawns for the Academy during the summer, but winter was mainly a time for hunting. Deer, rabbits, and ducks were fare for the family table, and fox furs provided cash income. Daylight was showing as they left, but the sky was gray, and the air carried a damp chill. Dick pulled the flaps of his hat down over his ears, fastened all the buttons on his winter coat, and pulled on the wool mittens that Mom had made just last week. He would like to have gone sliding with his friends today, but being asked to go hunting with his brother and Dad made him feel grown up, and it was a good feeling.

The hunters, Spot in the lead, walked across the back yard then through several neighboring yards before emerging on Water

Oakum Bay. Photo courtesy of Castine Historical Society

Street. They turned left and finally arrived at Grampa's house where their boat was kept. It was a "gunnin' boat," low to the water and painted gray to make it blend with the surroundings, about twelve feet long, and with a forward deck. Winky had named the boat *Effie* in honor of Dick's mother, the name painted in black letters on the stern. They carried the boat from behind the house down the beach and into the half-tide water of the Bagaduce River. Guns, ammunition and dinner box were all stowed under the forward deck, Dick and the dogs sat on the deck, Dad in the stern, and Linny took the middle seat to row. They headed up the river, past the two Negro Islands, and landed on the Brooksville shore at the old Castine-Brooksville ferry location. As they arrived, Dick heard the Castine town clock strike seven, sunrise time, but clouds covered that event. Dad had come here several weeks before to build a blind at the edge of the woods using driftwood and an old piece of canvas. This was where they would settle in to wait for ducks to land on the river. Linny slowly nosed the boat onto the beach where the dogs leaped off the bow, avoiding the cold river water. The three people stepped out over the side, their boots in ankle-deep. Winky took the gear out from under the deck, putting the boxes of shells in his coat pocket, then handing the guns and dinner box to Dick to carry. He and Linney picked up *Effie* to move her a short distance up the rocky beach and tied the painter around a sizable stone. Dick and the dogs started for the blind, the dogs in the lead.

Snow covered the ground above the high tide line, and as Spot arrived there he started running along the edge of the snow, nose to the ground and letting out an occasional bark. Wags followed close behind. Winkey moved up the beach to see what all the excitement was about, calling the dogs back before they tore off into the woods. There were three sets of tracks in the sand, two of them the dogs', and the third led off into the snow and woods beyond. Winkey knelt to inspect the tracks. They were very similar in both shape and size, but the one leading to the woods had several slight variations that were telling to Winkey's practiced eye—fox tracks. And they were fresh.

"C'mon, boys. Let's see if we can find this fox, then come back for ducks later." Winky picked up the rifle, Linny took the shotgun. They scrambled up the banking at the top of the beach and set off at a run through the snow. Spot was in the lead; Wags, Winkey and Linny followed close behind; and Dick was in the rear doing his best to keep up. As he made the turn around a large spruce tree, a protruding tree root snagged his boot, and he fell headlong into the wet snow and the mud underneath. By the time he had picked himself up and retrieved the lunch box, the others were out of sight. The tracks were there, and it would be possible to follow them, but the snow was deep for an eight-year-old, his boots were heavy, and he realized that catching up was probably not going to happen. He stood for a while looking at the tracks in the snow that disappeared into a dark woods. His mittens were wet, snow behind his collar was melting down his back, and he was all alone. Dick stifled a sob, wiped tears from his cheeks, then turned around and plodded back to the shore in hopes that Dad and Linny would not be gone long. There was a big log at the top of the beach near the blind from which Dick brushed the snow and sat to wait. The sky was gray, the river water was gray, and the trees on the other side were mostly gray and brown. A light snow had started to fall, and Dick was cold. He poured a cup of tea from the thermos thinking it would warm him. It didn't seem to help much. He ran up and down the beach waving his arms in an attempt to warm up, but that didn't seem to work either. He returned to the log, sat down, and tried to think that he was having a good time. It seemed like forever since Dad and Linny had disappeared into the woods pursuing that fox, but just now he heard the town clock struck eight. It had been only one hour since landing on the beach. Dick was wet, cold, and miserable. He turned and called toward the woods. "Dad?" No answer. He called again; still no answer.

The tide had come in enough that the boat was now floating. Dick untied the painter knot and pulled the line from under the rock thinking to move it farther up the beach, but there were no sizable rocks there to tie on to. On impulse, he climbed over the deck and into the boat, pulled in the painter, sat in the rowing seat and placed the oarlocks in their sockets. He had learned to row the summer before, not very well, but he thought he could make it back to Grampa's house. He set the oars in place, turned the boat, and started pulling for the Castine shore. Since he was sitting backwards in the boat, the blind and sitting-log were in his view. He could see the lunch box still on top of the log. Should he go back to get it? No. Dad and Linny would probably be mad that he left, but at least there would be something to eat while they waited. Grampa would know what to do about getting back to Brooksville to pick them up.

Dick turned in his seat to pick a destination on the opposite shore, and found that with the log directly astern, the bow was headed for a pile of rocks on a small point. He rowed for about five minutes, doing his best to keep the log astern, but when he turned around to look for the rock pile, it wasn't where it should be. The tidal current was sweeping him up the river, away from Castine. Dick pulled hard on the left oar to turn the boat so that it was headed nearly into the current and toward the channel separating the Castine mainland from the two Negro Islands. He continued rowing, hoping for the best and keeping an eye on the log, thinking that Dad and Linny might return. His progress was very slow, but when he reached the channel entrance, the current that had been opposing him slowed considerably such that the boat sped up relative to the land. The tide was close to high. Dick realized that the exertion of rowing had warmed him; in fact, he stopped rowing long enough to undo a few of the top buttons on his coat. By the time he reached Wescott Point, the tide had turned, and the current was now helping him on his journey toward Grampa's house.

This help was short-lived, however, as the water leaving Hatch's Cove pushed *Effie* back toward the middle of the river. The light breeze that had rippled the water surface earlier had now increased and that wind was coming out of the northeast, thus helping the current to push the boat toward Brooksville, nearly a mile away, but no longer visible due to the snow squall. Ripples had turned to waves which were slapping *Effie*'s side, resulting in water coming over the gunwale and into the boat. It sloshed around the bottom, not a good situation. If he stopped rowing to bail water, the wind and waves pushed him farther away from shore. So once again, he changed the boat's heading, this time directing it into the current toward the end of Mayo Point. This was not toward Grampa's house, but the bow was directed into the waves which were now deflected off to the sides rather than into the boat. Once he reached the Castine shore he could row parallel to the beach toward town. It would be a lee shore with no waves and beyond where the water leaving Hatch's Cove would affect his progress. In fact the tidal current would again be helping.

As *Effie*'s bow grounded on the sand beach of Mayo Point, Dick pulled the oars in and slumped forward. His arms ached, his shoulders ached, and he was sweating from the exertion. He took a few minutes to rest, then stood, and with an oar, pushed the boat off the beach and continued rowing. As he rounded the next point of land, Grampa's house came into view as the town clock struck nine.

Dick reached the shore in front of the house and grounded the boat so that it lined up with the series of logs that were set into the beach parallel to the river. Each log was about four feet long, partially buried, secured by stakes driven into the beach so that it didn't float away when submerged, and placed about three feet from its neighbors. The set of logs thus provided a pathway to pull small boats up the rocky beach without damaging their bottoms. Dick stepped out of *Effie*, retrieved the painter and started to pull the boat up over the logs. At first it was easy, and he made good progress, but as soon as the boat was clear of the water, he could barely move it. Suddenly Grampa was there, his hand on Dick's shoulder.

"What are you doing, Richard? Where have you been? Does your mother know where you are?"

Once again, Dick held back tears, and, with a flood of words, told what had happened. "And Dad and Linny are still over in

Brooksville. How can we get back there to pick 'em up?"

"They can just stay there for now. You're soakin' wet and shiverin'. Let's get back to the house and warm you up, then we'll figure out how to fetch 'em."

The old man and the boy pulled *Effie* to the top of the beach. Grampa tied the painter to a ring on the bulkhead. A few minutes later Dick was sitting in the kitchen easy chair in front of the Atlantic Clarion stove with his stocking feet resting on the open oven door. Grampa made a cup of hot cocoa along with a piece of toast with blueberry jelly, gave them to Dick, and then put his coat on.

"You sit there and warm up. I'm goin' next door to see if Woodrow will go in his outboard to find Winky and Linny. If he's willin', I'll go with him. You just stay put. There's more cocoa on the stove, and make more toast if you want."

Grampa put a few sticks of wood in the stove, then went out the door. Dick settled back into the cushions of the chair. It was warm and comfortable. Grampa's cat, Morsel, jumped up into his lap. Dick was tired. His head nodded, and both he and Morsel were soon asleep.

Meanwhile, the two fox hunters and their dogs had given up their pursuit. The quarry had crossed a marshy area where the ice was thick enough to hold a fox, but not a person. Each step they made broke through to water below. Fortunately the water depth was less than their boots' height. They turned back, discouraged, but at least with dry feet. The real problem showed up when they arrived at the duck blind. Dick was not there, and there was no boat, thus no way to get home. They did find the dinner box on a log and were glad to sit while eating a sandwich and drinking hot tea. Wags and Spot got the last few bites of sandwich. Thoughts of duck hunting were replaced with a discussion of where Dick was. Was he safe? And how could they get home? They could not see Castine from their current location, as the islands were in the way. More importantly, no one in Castine could see them. It was decided to walk south along the shoreline to the West Brooksville boat landing where Castine was visible, build a fire, and hope that someone would see them.

Their walk was along the shore of Lord's Cove where the town should be visible, but was now obscured by falling snow. There were a number of summer cottages next to the cove, but no one was in them at this time of year, so no help. A half hour later as they came around the next point, the snow squall had tapered, and Castine was in view. A small outboard-powered boat could be seen near Trott's Ledge and coming up the river toward them.

"That looks like Woodrow."

"I think it is, and there's someone with him. Is that Grampa?"

"Maybe. Take your coat off and start wavin' it. We've got to get their attention."

Linny removed his coat, turned it inside out to show the red lining, and waved it frantically over his head. Both Linny and Winky started shouting, although they knew it wouldn't help, as Woodrow would not hear over the din of his engine. In a few minutes, however, the boat turned and headed directly for the pair and their dogs on the shore. As it neared the beach, Woodrow shut off the engine, and the boat drifted toward them.

"Have you seen Dick? Did he get back to town?" There was real concern in Winky's voice.

His father called back. "He got back safe, no thanks to you."

"What is wrong with that boy? He just went off and left us. He's due for a lickin' when I get back." Winky's concern had turned to anger.

"Now, you just calm down. You're the ones who left him. He

was wet and freezin' cold. He had no choice except to row back, and he did a good job of takin' care of himself when you weren't there to do it. You should be proud of him. If anyone needs a lickin', it's you, and don't think I'm not able to do it." Grampa's tirade caught Winky by surprise, and he immediately backed off.

The ride back to town was mostly quiet except for the engine, but by the time they landed on the beach Winky was telling his father of the chase through the woods with Linny filling in details. They thanked Woodrow for his help, and then went to Grampa's house to find Dick at the kitchen table with another mug of hot cocoa and some Oreo cookies that he had found in the pantry. Grampa fed the Atlantic Clarion a few more sticks of wood, taking care not to step on the dogs who were curled up in front of the stove. He then filled three cups from the teapot on the back of the stove. The three of them, cups in hand, joined Dick and helped him finish the Oreos. The talk was of next Saturday's duck hunting trip. Grampa said he would go on that one.

The Dungeon

Glen was home for summer break following his junior year at Farmington State Teachers College. He really liked going to school, liked the courses and the people he met there. He had a part-time job at the library, played shortstop on the baseball team, and was in the band playing drums. He was eager to finish senior year and get on with his adult life, but for now it was good to be home and spend time with his family.

Glen was distressed that his father, for the first time, looked like an old man. His face was thin, his gray hair was sparse, and his back had a stoop that had not been there last year. Dad worked in the maintenance department at Maine Maritime Academy, mowing lawns, doing carpentry jobs, and helping where needed. He liked his job, mainly because of the variety, but much of it was hard physical work, and it was having an effect on his fifty-nine-year-old body, the one that had been pushed hard since age fifteen when his father died. Dad had quit school at that time and gone to work digging clams to support his mother and younger siblings.

Later he had worked at a variety of difficult jobs and felt fortunate to be hired by the Academy when it first opened. Glen's mother had worked for many years at the hospital, cleaning and helping in the kitchen. She had left that job last year and now cleaned houses for several retired couples and summer residents. She, too, was feeling the results of many years of hard work, but both parents took great pride that their son was in college and looking forward to a career of teaching.

Glen hoped to connect with a few high school friends who were still in town. Most of his classmates had left Castine to join the service or take jobs in Connecticut, and even Glen would likely not be here after this summer with a move to wherever his position as high school math teacher took him. He planned on that being somewhere other than Maine. But for now he would enjoy the summer with no academic deadlines, rather earn enough to pay next year's tuition, play golf, and relax. He liked working as a house-painter for Don Hutchins. This would be his third year at the job, and he was pretty good at it. The real test for a painter was window sashes, and Glen was nearly as fast as Don. His paint line sealed the intersection between glass and wood, and that line was straight; no blobs running out into the glass and no cleaning up after with a razor blade.

On this June day Glen had awakened at his usual six o'clock. It was raining, and his painting job didn't start until next week, so he went back to sleep. Several hours later, when finally arising, the rain had stopped, the sun was trying to show through breaking clouds, and Glen was ready for a day of leisure. Dad had left for work hours ago, and Mom had said last night that she was going to her sister's house for the day. Glen was on his own. What to do? He had dressed and walked downtown for coffee and donut at the drugstore. Right now he was outside the store, sitting on the bench next to the sidewalk with his back against the building. He was savoring a second cup of coffee and reading the *Bangor Daily News* he'd purchased at Willis Ricker's store. There was an encouraging article about the urgent need for new teachers.

This was a fine location to keep an eye on what was happening in downtown Castine. Across the street Gus Wardwell was loading baskets of groceries into the back of his Chevrolet wagon in preparation for delivering the orders that had been phoned in. Glen had worked at the market one summer while in high school. That job had convinced him that he didn't want to be a storekeeper, but driving the delivery van was fun, and it had led to his meeting that maid at the Paisley Cottage. She was three years older than Glen, but that didn't seem to matter. The two of them had spent one special August evening at Fort George. They sat together on top of the southwest rampart holding hands, watching the moon rise over Brooksville, and talking about what they wanted to do with their lives. There were serious hugs and kisses before the walk back to Paisley Cottage. Glen smiled as these thoughts ran through his mind. "What was her name? It was unusual... Pamela! That's it. Wonder where she is now." He had a pang of regret that they hadn't stayed in touch. There had been one exchange of letters in September, but nothing more.

These thoughts of past summer activities led to his wondering what he would find to do in his spare time this summer. The painting job was five and a half days a week, with Saturday afternoon, Sunday, and evenings free to play.

Charley Thayer came into view, walking on Water Street from the direction of his house at the bottom of Green that he shared with two other old bachelors. He turned left when he got to Main Street, heading for the town wharf. Charley was an old man, thin, not very tall, and with a face networked with wrinkles.

He had lost a leg many years ago, thus used a cane and hobbled along on an artificial limb. He usually dressed in a black suit with vest, an off-white shirt and gray tie. A black wool fisherman's hat with visor sat on his head. The town hired him during the summer to care for the public waterfront area, keeping the parking lot and wharf neat and cleaning the toilets. The latter were housed in a small white clapboarded building near Captain Ladd's freight dock. A casual observer might feel pity for Charley Thayer, but his face showed a sense of self-pride and determination, no self-pity.

Glen called out, "Hey, Charley. How's the waterfront?"

Charley turned. "So, you're home from school. Your father told me you'd be here for the summer." He continued down the hill toward the wharf. An extended conversation was not part of Charley's personality.

Two young boys appeared from behind Wardwell's Market, coming up the hill from Sea Street. Glen tried to think of who they were. "Familiar, but... Oh, the taller one is Eddie Leach's little brother. Leland, that's who it is. The other might be Lee Perkins' brother, but I don't know his name."

Leland and Keith had spent much of the morning on the waterfront at the buildings beyond Captain Ladd's wharf. They had climbed through an open window to the inside of the old sardine canning factory to retrieve a few can lids and explore the dim interior festooned with cobwebs. The rectangular can lids were printed "Dice's Head Brand" and included a picture of Dice's Head Lighthouse. The next stop had been to go aboard the *Helen*, an abandoned fishing boat lying on the beach next to the factory building. She had been there for years, paint peeling, wood rotting, and water coming in on rising tides and draining out on falling tides. That morning the tide was high, so the boys could only get on the main deck, but looking down through a hatch, rusty machinery showed in the murky water below. This was worth another visit at low tide. Finally, they had stopped in to see Ken Hooper at Hooper's Garage, the local Ford agent. The business was located in the east end of the sardine factory building. The structure, like the *Helen*, was slowly decaying. Merton, Ken's father, had recently purchased property at the corner of Main and Water streets, across from Wardwell's Market, and a new garage was planned for that location. Keith, especially, liked cars and wanted to know if Ken knew what the 1949 Fords would look like. There had been little change in the shape since the mid-1930s.

"They're gonna be completely different, very modern. You won't recognize 'em." Keith's parents owned a Chevrolet and Leland's family had a Plymouth. Both boys felt a loyalty toward the family vehicles, but those brands had six-cylinder engines. Fords had the option of a V8, and that was hard to ignore in spite of that loyalty.

Keith and Leland crossed Main Street and sat on the edge of the sidewalk by the drugstore entrance. Glen could hear their conversation, but tried to ignore it and continued reading. The Sports page had an article about the Red Sox and their game with the Yankees tonight. It was to be broadcast on WABI radio, and Glen, a Red Sox fan, planned to listen.

Keith asked Leland if he knew what day it was. "It's Monday. School's been over for nearly a week."

"But do you know what date it is?"

"Ummm, no. I guess around the twentieth. Why?"

"It's the twenty-first, longest day of the year, and tonight's when the drummer boy plays up at Fort George."

For those not familiar with Castine, Fort George, located on the hill above the village, is a level area of several acres surrounded by an earthen wall and a dry moat outside of that. There is a masonry dungeon in one corner. The fort was built by British troops who occupied Castine during the American Revolution. For Glen, Keith and Leland, Fort George was important because the level area was as the town's baseball field. A local legend holds that when the British departed, they locked the dungeon, but inadvertently a drummer boy was left inside. He played his drum hoping to attract someone's attention to save him, but that didn't happen. He died three days later. Each year, on the anniversary of his death, for those brave enough to go to the fort at midnight, his ghost can be heard playing the drum.

Leland replied to Keith's assertion. "I don't think that's tonight, it happens at the full moon in August. My father told me about it, said he and my uncle Horace went there one year and heard the drum. They about peed their pants and ran all the way home."

"Well, my brother told me tonight at midnight's when it happens. I think we should go up and see if the ghost is there tonight. Want to?"

"Yeah, we can try. I don't think it's the right night, but it'd be fun. Oh... My mother won't let me stay out that late. She won't even let me out after supper."

"How about if you stay at my house tonight?" Keith asked.

"Will your mother let us out?"

"Prob'ly not, but we won't tell her about it. We can climb out my bedroom window onto the porch roof, then climb down the maple tree that's beside the house. I've done it before, and it's easy. We'll go up to the fort to get there a little before twelve and sit on the bank outside the dungeon."

"Okay, I'll ask my mother, but I still think it happens in August," said Leland.

The boys got up from their curbside seats and started up Main, passing Glen as they went. Glen had listened in on much of the boys' conversation and had an idea for his evening's entertainment. His head was full of thoughts on how to make it happen, and he talked the plan over with himself. "I'll need a drum, and Willis Ricker probably has one. He's got lots of instruments left over from when he directed the town band. He'd lend me a drum, but I'll probably have to tell him what I want it for. Lucky I just bought a paper there, puts me in a better position for a loan." Glen took the coffee cup back inside the drugstore and put it on the counter. Mr. Ricker's store was the next stop.

That evening, after supper, Glen helped his mother clean up the kitchen and then they joined his father in the living room. The baseball game started at seven thirty, and the three of them sat near the large wood-cased RCA radio to listen. All three were Red Sox fans, knew the players, their strengths, weaknesses and batting averages. Baseball was the main thing that they now had in common, and a night game gave an opportunity to spend an enjoyable few hours together. That night the Red Sox won, 5 to 4. The game was over by ten, and the parents went to bed soon after that.

Glen thumbed through last week's issue of *The Saturday Evening Post*, mainly looking at cartoons, then made a tour through the kitchen. The refrigerator yielded leftover ham that he combined with three biscuits from the back of the bread box. They were several days old, but tasted fine after being put through the toaster, buttered, and topped with ham. He got his jacket and a flashlight from the front hall closet and went to the garage to retrieve the canvas bag with drum inside that he had hidden earlier in the day. He left the house, closing the door quietly behind him. It was a beautiful time for a walk. The sky was clear, and the air held the chill of a Maine summer night. He fastened several of the buttons on his jacket. A half-circle of the moon gave enough light to show his way, and the Big Dipper hovered over his right shoulder as he walked across the ninth hole of the golf course. He crossed Back Shore Road, then down into the dry moat and up the steep earthen wall of the fort, encountering thorny blackberry bushes in the process. Glen took several minutes at the dungeon entrance when the thought crossed his mind: "Maybe I don't want to do this." But he mustered courage, switched on the flashlight, and lowered his head to enter.

The dungeon was a tunnel made of stone and brick with an arched ceiling that was not quite high enough for Glen to stand upright. The total length was only about fifteen feet, but a bend part way through obscured the end from view at the entrance. At that far end a small opening led to a hemispherical room about five feet in diameter, which supposedly was the gunpowder stor-

The "dungeon" at Fort George. Photo courtesy of Castine Historical Society

age area. Glen's flashlight beam showed discarded beer and pop bottles, candy wrappers and cigarette butts. Not a pleasant place to spend much time, but more to the point, it was spooky. Glen didn't believe in ghosts, or thought they were harmless if they did exist. But you never know what a disgruntled ghost might do. He took a deep breath and entered, but then immediately stopped. Was that a noise from the back recess? He stood, stooped, not moving, not even breathing. There was no noise, no movement, just his imagination playing on his fears. He went forward, picking his way among the debris, around the bend, and to the far corner so he was not visible from the entrance. The opening to the gunpowder room was close by on his right, but he had no interest in crawling onto that cobweb-infested space. There was a short piece of log that he upended and moved to the farthest corner to use as a seat. Glen took the drum out of the canvas bag, positioned it between his knees, switched off the flashlight and settled in to wait. Hopefully, those two boys would be along soon.

It was very quiet and very dark; cold and damp; unsettling. As Glen sat waiting, he had an uneasy feeling that someone or something was close by. The air seemed even colder than when he had arrived, and in spite of his jacket and brave thoughts, a shiver went up his back. "Come on, Glen, get hold of yourself. There's no ghost, and you're here to have fun scaring those two kids." He buttoned his jacket the rest of the way, tucked his hands under his armpits, and sat hunched over with his head inside his collar, looking like a turtle.

Leland had gotten permission to spend the night at Keith's house, and after supper they had listened to the Red Sox game. Keith was not much interested in baseball, but he knew that Leland was, so he did the right thing and pretended to enjoy the game. Leland loved baseball. It was more important to him than almost anything else, and his ambition was to play professionally. Pitching for the Red Sox would be the ultimate life experience, and Leland fully expected to achieve that.

When the game was over the boys said their goodnights to Keith's parents and went upstairs, yawning and seeming to be ready to sleep. In fact they were keyed up to the point that sleep was not on their minds at all. To move time along, they sat on opposite sides of a table in Keith's room, talked, and worked on assembling a Piper Cub model airplane. It was the kind that one could buy at the drugstore for twenty-five cents. Parts for the frame were printed on thin sheets of balsa wood. These were cut out using a single-edge razor blade, and then assembled into wings, fuselage, and tail section using glue. A rubber band propulsion system was installed inside the fuselage. The next steps involved gluing tissue paper to the outside of the components and putting water on the paper. When the paper dried, it shrank, resulting in a tight skin. Next, the wings and tail pieces were glued to the fuselage, and the plane was ready to fly.

At eleven o'clock they heard Keith's parents climb the stairs. Keith turned off his bedroom light, fearing it would show under the door to the hall, and they waited to hear the parents' bedroom door close. At eleven thirty they put on jackets, climbed out the window to the porch roof, and climbed down the maple tree. It was, as Keith had said earlier, easy.

The walk up Pleasant Street took them past the Academy dormitory in front of which stood a large flagpole, reputed to be the mast from an old sailing ship. Mounted on the base of the pole was a ship's bell which, when students were in residence, was rung every half hour by a student on watch. (The number of strikes tells the time, sort of. The system used is based on a ship's four-hour watch cycle. So, for instance, at noon "eight bells" were rung; a half hour later, at twelve thirty, "one bell"; at one o'clock it was "two bells", and so on. The number increases by one for each half hour until four o'clock when eight bells again sound and the cycle starts again.) The young boys of Castine found that it was great night-time fun to hide behind bushes close to the flagpole, wait until the watch stander had rung the bell and gone back inside, then dash across the lawn and ring the bell madly, preferably more than eight times. Students would pour out of the dormitory and chase the offenders through the darkness. As far as was known, none was ever caught. On this night, with all students away from campus on a short summer break and no one to give chase, there was no interest in ringing the bell.

Keith and Leland continued toward Fort George, went through the opening in the wall on the southeast side and turned left. When they got to the dungeon their flashlight beam illuminated the inside: trash on the dirt floor, moss on the walls, and water drops hanging from the ceiling. It was a scary sight, and they had no trouble deciding not to go inside. They sat on the ground near the entrance, leaned back against the steep earthen walls of the fort, and waited.

Glen, still seated at the far end of the tunnel, had heard them coming and seen the flashlight beam on the wall to his right. For a moment he thought they might come in and discover him. He thought about pulling his jacket up over his head and jumping at them as they came around the corner, but then heard "no way am I goin' in there." He waited until he thought it might be midnight, then started playing the drum, softly at first.

"Rat-a-tat-tat, rat-a-tat-tat, rat-a-tat-tat."

Then a bit louder.

"RAT-A-TAT-TAT, RAT-A-TAT-TAT, RAT-A-TAT-TAT."

Before the second round was finished he heard the boys

scream and the sound of running feet. He continued to play a few more rounds, then stopped to listen. All was quiet. He waited a bit before emerging from the dungeon. He set the drum on a rock, climbed the embankment, and, lying on his stomach, peered over the top and down toward Pleasant Street. The boys were standing under a street light looking up at the fort, gesturing and talking rapidly, but Glen couldn't understand the words. They soon turned and hurried down the hill toward Keith's house. Glen guessed that he would hear about the drummer boy's appearance when he arrived downtown tomorrow morning.

He went back down the embankment to retrieve the drum, and as he leaned down, the town clock started striking midnight. At the sound of the bell, Glen thought, "So much for that old story about the drummer boy, he's not here, at least not tonight." He picked up the drum and sticks, and had just gotten them back into the canvas bag when the twelfth bell of midnight struck. At that moment a sound came from the dungeon, the sound of a drum, very faint at first, but gaining volume. Glen stood petrified. He told his feet to run, but they did not move. He looked up, and at the far end of the dungeon a faint glow showed, the shape almost like a person, two legs, a torso, and a head. The sound of the drum became deafening, and the light became brighter. Glen's body finally responded. He picked up the canvas bag and ran. He ran faster than ever before, even when base-running. He scrambled up and over the northeast side of the fort wall, down the embankment, through the blackberry bushes, across the moat, across Backshore Road, and onto the golf course headed for home. He didn't see the moon or the Big Dipper. He didn't think about what a pleasant evening it was. He just ran home.

When Glen returned the drum the next day, Mr. Ricker asked about events of the previous night. "Did the boys show up? Did you scare 'em? What happened to your face? It's all scratched up."

Glen told a bit of what happened with the boys, but did not continue with what he saw and heard at midnight. As he was about to leave, Mr. Ricker said, "So, do you think the drummer boy's ghost is there?"

Glen looked at the old man. Mr. Ricker's sly expression hinted that he knew more of last night's happenings than Glen had told, but he replied, "I don't know. He wasn't supposed to be there last night anyway. Maybe I'll go back in August and see what happens."

"Well, if you do that, let me know. I'd like to go along with you."

As Glen walked down Main Street headed for coffee at the drugstore, the thought occurred: "Could he have...? No, not Willis Ricker. He's the town's first selectman, a business owner, used to be in the state legislature, very conservative, a pillar of the community. Besides, he's too old to do anything like that... Isn't he? Maybe he's seen the ghost, had the same experience I had last

Willis Ricker at his store, Ricker's Variety Store, with Maine Maritime Academy students. Photo courtesy of Castine Historical Society

night. Wants to see it again, but not alone. Still... that look he gave me. He knows something he didn't tell about."

Glen did not go back to Fort George on the night of the full moon in August, nor did he ever tell anyone about his June twenty-first night there. He made a point of not going to the fort after dark, and even when playing baseball there was reluctant to play center field, that location being near the dungeon.

Walker's Pond 1951

It was mid-April of their seventh grade year when Jay, Harold and Don, anticipating spring after a long winter, decided on another camping trip to Walker's Pond. There was no Boy Scout troop in Castine to organize activities like this, but Jay's father, John, was an outdoor enthusiast with hunting and fishing high on his list of good things to do. He also thought camping was a fine activity for boys, but was past the age where he wanted to sleep in a tent. He appointed himself the adviser.

Last year's outing had been for one night, not nearly enough time. After making a list of things they wanted to do, the boys thought three nights seemed reasonable. They would arrive on a Monday afternoon in time to set up camp, and come home the following Thursday morning. The two days between would allow swimming, fishing, hiking, and dining on all of the camp food menus they had come up with. All three boys were reasonably competent at cooking over a campfire, so the meals would be more than just opening cans and heating the contents. Their three breakfasts were to be scrambled eggs, french toast, and pancakes, with bacon included for all. A box of Bisquick would be the basis for making pancakes, and it would also allow for biscuits to be part of evening meals. They had previously found that biscuit batter could be cooked in a fry pan with butter as the cooking oil, something like frybread. It was delicious. The three dinners would be hamburgers, baked beans with hotdogs, and red flannel hash, the latter being a mixture of hamburger, potatoes, onions and beets cooked in a fry pan. A salt shaker and large bottle of catsup were the only condiments. Jay's mother, Doris, looked over their list.

"You need vegetables. The only thing you've got is a can of beets, and that's not enough. I'll get some carrots and radishes. Those are easy to fix. You can eat them raw. Do you all like those?"

Harold and Don nodded agreeably, but Jay said something about catsup being a vegetable. Doris would hear none of that. There were only two lunches, and they were easy: peanut butter and jelly sandwiches plus a large bag of potato chips. The suggestion that potato chips were vegetables also did not impress Doris.

On a Monday afternoon in mid-June, after school was out for the year, the three boys met at Jay's house. Each brought his share of food and camping equipment plus extra clothes, fishing rod and a sleeping bag. Jay had a real sleeping bag, bought at L.L. Bean and rated for temperatures down to thirty degrees. Harold and Don had each made one by folding an old blanket and sewing up the bottom and side. The result was something that resembled the real thing, but was not rated for thirty degrees. Harold also brought his telescope. They had studied astronomy in science class this year, and he thought that Walker's Pond would be a good place to observe the planets and the full moon that was due that first night. John, who took cooking seriously, reviewed the items being taken and added a large cast iron fry pan. The little aluminum versions that came in the camp kits that each boy had were, in his opinion, completely useless.

All of this gear was loaded into the trunk of the John's 1949 Buick Roadmaster, and the expedition was under way by three o'clock. They followed Route 166 out of Castine, turned right onto Route 199 and passed through Penobscot village. Smoke was coming out of the brick kiln building, indicating that bricks were being fired. All was quiet at the canning factory as it was too early in the season to harvest the local fruits and vegetables that were processed there. There was some back-seat talk about stopping at the Bagaduce Lunch, but that idea was vetoed. The final leg of the trip was down a narrow gravel road to an east-facing beach. It was on private land, but the owners allowed local people to picnic and swim there. What no one in the car realized was that the land had been sold the previous fall, and that the new owners had different ideas on how the property would be used.

John helped the boys unload their gear and drove off, leaving them to set up camp. They found a secluded spot on a rise of land to the right of the beach that had a stand of tall pine trees and a line of low bushes separating it from the beach area. It had been used for camping before as evidenced by a fire pit and several smooth level spots for setting up tents. An hour later the campsite was all in order and the boys were enjoying a late afternoon swim in the pond.

The word pond is sometimes thought to mean a small body of fresh water—muddy fresh water as in "frog pond." Walker's Pond is not that. It is about two miles long, a half mile wide, and shaped like a boot. Think Italy, but with the toe facing right instead of left. The beaches are sandy, the water is clear, and the temperature is comfortable for swimming by mid-June; comfortable that is, for twelve-year-old boys whose alternative is Maine coast ocean water. The land around Walker's Pond is not highly developed and much of the shoreline is wooded. The pond length is oriented north-south, and the boys' campsite, on the western shore, faced Caterpillar Hill, the sunrise, and the full moonrise.

That first evening passed uneventfully. The campers built a fire and prepared a supper of hamburgers, potato chips, Nesbitt's orange soda, and even a few carrots and radishes. For dessert they worked on a bag of chocolate chip cookies. The sun went below the hill behind them at about seven o'clock, but kept shining on Caterpillar Hill in the east until after eight. Shortly after that light disappeared, the full moon rose over the hill. It was huge. While Jay and Don sat by the campfire and talked about 1948 Fords, Harold retrieved his telescope from the back of the tent and aimed it at the moon. He studied the surface: craters, plains, and mountains. He was intrigued by what he saw and called to the others.

"Look at this. You can see the craters. That's where meteors have crashed into the moon. It'd be fun to go there and walk around exploring."

He handed the telescope to Don who peered through the instrument. "There's a crater like that in Arizona. I saw pictures of it in *National Geographic*. It's big, about ten miles across, I think. You could go there and explore."

"You think people will ever go to the moon?"

Jay, still waiting for his turn, had an opinion. "No. That's impossible. Don't you remember? It's boiling hot during the day and way below zero at night. And there's not even any air. They'd die."

Don attempted to salvage the trip to the moon. "They could wear insulated suits and take a bunch of scuba tanks."

"It's way too hot and way too cold for any kind of insulated suit. And do you know how many scuba tanks it would take just to get there and back? There wouldn't be room for 'em all in the rocket."

Harold said, "Well, I think they'll send rockets there. If they can't get people to go, they could put a television camera inside pointed out a window so we could see what it's like."

The moon observation and conversation went on until that topic was pretty well covered. By then it was completely dark, and the telescope was pointed at some of the bright stars. They didn't seem very interesting, just dots of light, but then a larger circle was found, and it seemed to have several small dots close by that did not look like stars. This could be a planet with its moons, and the three agreed that it was probably Jupiter. As the evening hours mounted, the air temperature at Walker's Pond went down, and the boys finished their first day there huddled around the campfire eating chocolate chip cookies.

The tent that Don brought was new, purchased at a hardware store in Brewer. The unopened box claimed it had room for three, but after assembling it, the question was "three what?" Not three twelve-year-old boys, let alone adults. The tent was about six feet wide and seven feet long, perhaps sufficient space for three people, but the pup tent shape resulted in sloping walls so that the effective width was more like five feet. After some discussion about who would sleep where, Harold, the shortest, crawled all the way in to the far end and slept sideways. Jay and Don took more conventional spaces with their heads just barely inside the front door flaps. It was a long night with little sleep and a lot of talk. Harold and Don were both cold in their homemade sleeping bags, and got up in the night to retrieve jackets. Harold complained about feet invading his space.

Sunrise was at five o'clock, although Caterpillar Hill blocked the official event. The boys were up shortly after first light, and by the time the sun's warming rays reached them they had finished a breakfast of bacon and pancakes, all the time crowded around the fire to ward off the lingering night-time chill. They were eager for a day of adventure in spite of their lack of sleep.

The rest of the morning went as planned. Several hours of fishing resulted in two small specimens of unknown variety that were cleaned and put in the ice box to supplement dinner. These salt water town boys knew about pollock, mackerel, sculpin, tomcod, and dogfish, the kinds that could be caught off the Castine town dock, but freshwater fish were new to them. By mid morning it was warm enough that they switched from fishing to swimming. Several carloads of people, mostly mothers with young children, arrived to swim and picnic. It was early afternoon before Jay reminded the other two that it was past lunchtime. They made their way back to the hidden campsite, and soon after lunch the other people packed up and left. Quiet returned to the beach.

It was hot. The June sun, at its high point for the year, had been warming this protected shoreline all morning. The first hot-bug of the season sang, and all thoughts of an afternoon hike were put away. Each boy found a shady spot with pine needles for a seat and a friendly pine tree for a backrest. Jay, with his pad of paper and pencil, started drawing. He planned to be an artist and was getting an early start on his career. Don took out his jackknife and whittled aimlessly on pieces of pine limb. Harold's shady spot afforded a view of the opposite shore which he studied intently using his telescope. There was supposed to be a girls' camp there, but apparently it had not yet started for the summer. Harold could find no sign of activity.

This peaceful scene was interrupted by the arrival of another car, and it stopped at a location that was visible to Harold through the branches and leaves of the adjacent bushes. He swung the telescope in that direction and whispered to Jay and Don.

"That car's got a Québec license plate... and there's five people got out. Two men and two women and one girl."

"Is she good-lookin'?"

"I can't see her face. She's walkin' in the other direction. Now she's gone into the bushes there. I can hear 'em talkin', but can't understand 'em."

"Of course you can't, they're from Québec. They speak French."

Harold turned around, flapping one arm and putting an index finger to his lips. "Be quiet, we don't want 'em to know we're here."

"Why not?"

"Because they're takin' their clothes off, changin' into bathin' suits right there on the beach."

Don and Jay scrambled from their places under the trees, crept over to the bushes, and peeked through the branches. Sure enough, the four adults were stripping about two hundred yards away.

"Where's the girl?"

"She's over in the bushes. Must be changin' there."

A discussion followed about sharing the telescope, but Harold was not eager to share.

"It's my telescope. You should have brought your own."

In the end he did share, but too late. By the time Jay and Don got their turns, everyone was attired in modest bathing suits, including the girl who had emerged from her private changing space. She was older than the boys by perhaps a few years, had light brown hair, a trim figure, and was very pretty. Jay said he'd never seen a French girl who wasn't pretty. Harold said he'd never seen a French girl.

The trio stayed quietly hidden for the next half hour while the visitors swam. There was great anticipation of the changing back to dry clothes, but when the time came the pretty French girl went back to the bushes at the far end of the beach. The four adults retrieved their clothes and towels from the car, but then stayed there with the car between them and the boys. There was serious disappointment at the campsite that afternoon as they watched the car from Québec move up the gravel road, leaving only a cloud of dust that drifted slowly toward them. From the east, a bank of clouds moved across the sky in their direction.

That evening, at about nine o'clock—after finishing a red flannel hash supper supplemented by two small fish, dishes washed, the bag of chocolate chip cookies emptied, the last three sodas finished, and a conversation started about girls—flashes of lightning appeared to the north followed by thunder rumblings.

Jay commented, "If you count seconds, one one-thousand, two one-thousand, and so on, between when you see the lightning and when you hear the thunder, that's how far away it is in miles."

Don didn't think so. "Those jet planes from Dow (Air Force Base in Bangor) that fly over Castine? When you hear a sonic boom it means they're going faster than sound, and that's six hundred miles an hour. That's... ten miles a minute, or... one sixth of a mile in a second. So it takes six seconds for sound to travel one mile." Don, a potential engineer, liked math.

Another lightning flash and they counted nine seconds to the sound of thunder, so the storm was either one and one half miles away or nine miles away, depending on whose theory was used. Harold, who seemed not interested in the topic, interrupted.

"It's gonna rain. We've got to get our stuff inside the tent."

There followed a scramble to sort out what could get wet (cans of food, fishing gear, dishes, etc.) and what needed to stay dry (clothes, matches, some food items). The latter were stowed in the back of the tent, Harold's sleeping space. While they were working, the time between lightning flashes and thunder booms shortened, and a light rain began to fall just as the last items were safely inside. The boys crowded into the tent and watched as the light rain became a downpour, the lightning closing in to turn darkness to daylight, and thunder seeming to shake the ground under them. It was just scary enough to be exciting. The rain eventually tapered to a light drizzle and continued for most of the night. The trio found that the tent material was mostly waterproof unless something rubbed against it, and with three of them sharing the inside of this very small tent with gear piled in the back, they rubbed against it in numerous places. Water came through and ran down the side to the tent floor. Adding to the problem, the zipper for the mosquito netting jammed and would not close. The tent was soon filled with buzzing biting insects. And it was cold. None of the occupants found any humor in their situation, and there was very little sleep. Three grumpy campers got up at four o'clock. The rain had stopped and patches of blue sky were showing. Perhaps there was hope after all.

A supply of dead tree branches to be used for campfires had been gathered the day before and piled against one of the large pines near the tent. The tree branches above had shed some of the rain, but the firewood was wet. Harold said that his father, a fur trapper and experienced woodsman, had told him that no matter how wet everything might be you could always start a fire using bark from dead birch trees. Fortunately, several of those trees were lying on the ground nearby, and Harold harvested a supply of bark from the trunks. He arranged this at the bottom of the fire pit, then added a layer of small pine branches, the driest ones available, and finally put several larger pieces of wood on top. A single match touched to the birch bark resulted in an immediate substantial flame and black smoke curling up through the wood above. Within minutes the campers were crouched around a warming fire. Jay, the breakfast cook, took over, and the group was soon eating bacon and French toast. The misery of the night before was just a bad memory.

The morning routine was similar to that of the day before: fishing, swimming, and a lunch of peanut butter and jelly sandwiches with potato chips. They drank lake water because the soda was gone. Even worse, there were no cookies left. They had been consumed with no thought of the future. The boys tried pouring Log Cabin maple-flavored syrup over pieces of bread, but it was not a good substitute for chocolate chip cookies. Jay reminisced about ice cream cones, but that did not help.

It was decided to take a hike. They headed north along the edge of the pond thinking to walk on beaches when available and wade or even swim when necessary. Harold was in the lead. Harold loved to run and was usually in the lead. Right now, though, he was not running, rather standing. He bent over, reached down, and then stood with his hand up clasping something between thumb and index finger.

"I found a quarter!"

Don and Jay hurried to catch up, but Don stopped and dropped to the sand. "I've got a dime and a nickel. Someone must have been walking here with a hole in his pocket."

The next ten minutes were spent searching the beach, and in the end they had found eighty-seven cents. Jay, still thinking about ice cream, said, "Down at Robinson's Drug Store, double-decker cones are twenty cents."

"What are you talking about? We're in Brooksville. We can't go to the drugstore."

"I know that, but there's a grocery store in Buck's Harbor, you know—Eddy's Market. I'm pretty sure they've got ice cream, and it's not far. We came by it on the way over here. Remember?

We must have enough money to buy three ice cream cones, and we can walk there."

The Eddy's Market that the boys knew was an extension of the store in Buck's Harbor. The store's owner, Eddy, had a delivery truck with a box mounted on the back the size of a small building. Steps that could be pulled out from under the truck and folded down to the ground gave access to a door leading to the inside, which was lined with shelves and bins. They held a variety of canned goods, bakery items, fruits, vegetables, candy and drinks. Both sides of the outside were painted with "Eddy's Market, A Store to Your Door." Eddy had several routes through neighboring towns, including Castine. Most of his customers lived in rural areas, but there were a few who lived in villages, including Harold's mother.

The boys left their camp site and started up the gravel road armed with eighty-seven cents and the determination to walk to Eddy's Market. Their perception of it not being very far was skewed by having covered the distance in a car going forty miles an hour. In truth, it was nearly three miles, and, like yesterday, the day was hot. After about twenty minutes, it dawned on them that it was a long walk for ice cream cones, and it was decided to hitchhike. Over the next hour only three cars went by, and they did just that, went by. It was a sorry-looking trio that arrived at the store. Their shirts were wet, sweat was dripping from their chins, and even Harold was moving slowly. The man behind the counter looked up as they entered. It was Eddy.

"What are you boys doing here? You're from Castine, aren't you? My, you look beat. Must have walked all the way over here."

They explained about camping at Walker's Pond, about running out of soda and cookies, really needing ice cream cones, and finding money on the beach. After considering prices and their financial situation, they settled on three double-decker ice cream cones (twenty cents each), three bottles of pop (five cents each), and a small bag of potato chips (ten cents). There was still two cents left which was used to buy two Tootsie Rolls. Eddy threw in a third. The campers took all of this to a bench on the porch at the front of the store and spent a lovely half-hour sitting in the shade, resting and eating all of their purchases.

As they were preparing to walk back to the pond, a man came out of the store carrying two bags of groceries. He looked at the boys. "Eddy tells me you're goin' to Walker's Pond. I'm headed that way. You can ride along if you're willin' to sit in the back of my truck. I'll let ya off at the end of Herrick Road."

The man was probably sixty years old with gray hair showing below his oil-stained tan cap, and the stubble of a beard outlined his deeply tanned face. Startling blue eyes and an easy smile made him immediately likable. He was wearing a red and black checked flannel shirt on this hot day, denim overalls, and a pair of hip boots with the tops rolled down to the knees. These were sometimes called "Deer Isle sneakers," necessary footwear for any self-respecting clam digger.

No time was wasted with the boys' acceptance of his offer, and they filed along behind as he crossed the street toward a 1936 Chevrolet pickup. The truck was probably dark green when new, but now had a patina of rusty red overspreading the paint. One of the rear fenders had a substantial dent and was hanging from two loose bolts near the top. As they approached, the boys could see a very large black dog sitting in the driver's seat and looking out through the rear window at them. They climbed over the tailgate into the back of the truck, pushed aside several galvanized buckets that smelled of fish bait, and sat on a coil of manila rope that was in the middle of the truck bed. The man checked to see that the tail-gate was latched, and then got into the cab, urging the dog to the passenger side of the seat and putting his groceries in the middle.

The truck started with a roar and a cloud of blue smoke rolled out behind it. There was the obvious need for a new muffler and a ring job, but the engine ran smoothly, and they were soon going past Condon's Garage and up the hill out of Buck's Harbor at what seemed like a high rate of speed. It really was only about thirty miles an hour, but the engine noise, the wind, and the dented fender flapping and banging on the side of the truck made it seem much faster. It was a wonderful ride to Herrick Road. When the truck stopped, the boys got out and thanked the man and watched as he drove away. Don said he'd love to have a truck like that, but a Ford with a flat-head V8 would be even better.

Supper that night was later than usual. It was an easy meal to prepare: an open can of beans heated on a flat rock at the edge of the fire and hotdogs roasted on the end of sticks. Late afternoon had seen the arrival of three cars from which spilled a dozen or more people, both adults and children. They seemed to be members of several families, perhaps all related. They had built a roaring fire to cook clams and lobsters, the adults were drinking beer, and everyone was having a noisy good time. As the sun was about to disappear behind the hill behind them, a fourth car, a large black sedan, came down the gravel road, raising a cloud of dust. It stopped on the grass at the top of the beach, and two men got out, shouting at the party-makers below. The boys came out from behind the line of bushes that concealed their campsite to see what was happening, only to be seen by the younger of the two new arrivals.

"What are you doing there? You're not supposed to be here. Get out!"

Jay assumed the role of spokesman. "We're campin' here, up in these pine trees. We've done it before, and it's okay."

"I don't know who told you it's okay because it's not. We bought this property last fall. It's ours, and it's private. There's no camping and there's no one allowed here. It's private property. Now pack up your stuff and get out before I call the sheriff."

A pause, then, "Yes, sir, if you say so."

The other group was apparently receiving a similar message, but their response was not as passive as Jay's. A shouting match was going on at the beach, and the man who had accosted the boys turned his attention there to join the fray. For a few minutes it looked as if a scuffle would occur, and the boys stayed to watch, anticipating some action. One cooler head in the partying group took over, however, and violence was averted. After lengthy discussion, the revelers put out the fire and started to pack their picnic gear, showing obvious reluctance. Mumbled comments about "summer complaints" and "go back to New Jersey" could be heard. The boys crept back through the bushes and started to pack their camp gear.

It was dark by the time the camp was dismantled and pieces carried up to Herrick Road. A white farm house nearby showed lights, and the boys went there in hopes of using a telephone. In response to their knock a dog barked, then a woman opened the door. A black Labrador retriever with a wagging tail squeezed by to greet the boys. The woman and her husband had heard the noise of the shouting match on the beach, and she wanted to know details. Of course the boys were eager to explain, and she was eager to hear. Said she had been told by the new owners not to walk her dog down the road to the pond any more. The husband interrupted this direction of conversation.

"I think this whole problem can be sorted out. Those people just moved up here, and in New Jersey they have to be like that. There's too many people down there. I've met 'em, and they're basically nice enough, just don't understand about how to live outside the city. I took a bag of lettuce and radishes from our garden over to 'em yesterday. Thought I'd show 'em about sharing and being neighborly. They seemed surprised, but asked me in, and we had a nice talk. I can get 'em to come around to how we do things here."

The lady of the house lacked optimism. "Well, maybe you can do that. I hope so... but I doubt it."

The discussion continued about the new landowners while Jay called his father. A short time later the boys were sitting on piles of camping gear by the side of Herrick Road waiting for a ride home. While swatting mosquitoes, they watched the nearly full moon shimmer on Walker's Pond as it rose over Caterpillar Hill.

Castine's July 4th running race, 1956, six years after the camping trip at Walker's Pond. At right is Harold Hatch receiving his first place trophy from Selectman James Sawyer. At left is second place winner Dale Lincoln.

Photo courtesy of Castine Historical Society

The Rowboat

The family boat, a thirteen-foot rowing craft, was built on Eagle Island about 1930, the result of generations of island dwellers perfecting a design both seaworthy and easy to row. The shear line, starting high at the bow, dipping to a low point amidships, then rising slightly to the stern, was most pleasing to the eye. The transom was an hourglass shape, although wider than on some boats to allow for a generous beam of a little over four feet. Her carvel planking was native cedar, about one-half inch thick, and the ribs, stem and keel were all white oak. Every spring young Dave scraped and sanded, primed bare spots, and painted the hull white, inside and out. The gunwale, seats, floor boards and oars were all painted light gray. She did not have a name, at least none painted on the stern, but was always referred to as "The Rowboat." Once in the water she responded to a stroke of the oars by gliding forward and holding a steady course. She was a lovely boat to see and to row.

Dave's mother was not enthused about her seventeen-year-old

son's expeditions in the rowboat, and for good reason. She thought the size to be appropriate for use on the Bagaduce River but, in spite of those Eagle Islanders, not on Penobscot Bay where waves frequently grew to heights that could easily swamp a boat of that size. However, Dave did not hesitate to row across the bay, nearly ten miles of open water, to Belfast or to Deer Isle or to Buck's Harbor. Also, in 1946 life jackets (or PFDs as they are now officially known) were not usually carried on small boats, and Dave's rowboat was no exception. It was not that boaters ignored safety rules, it's just that the rules did not exist, and apparently it did not occur to most that life jackets might be useful at certain times.

On this July Sunday morning, Dave's only day off from work, his alarm clock sounded at four forty-five. He had covered it with a towel to muffle the sound, thus hoping that his parents would not hear it. He wanted to be out of the house before they awoke. Breakfast was a bowl of cereal and a banana. Two peanut butter sandwiches and an apple went into a paper bag to take along as lunch. He filled his army surplus canteen with water, added two Milk Bone dog biscuits to the lunch bag, wound his Westclox pocket watch, and tied a sweatshirt around his waist. A quick scribbled note was left on the kitchen table: "I've gone for a row, probably across the river." Mom would interpret "the river" as Bagaduce River, but it could mean Penobscot River. At the last minute, he remembered to slip a small compass into his pocket and left the house at five thirty.

Obadiah, the family dog, was at his side as he walked down Green Street toward Dennett's Wharf where The Rowboat was kept. Obadiah was a large black and white dog, the son of a Newfoundland mother and a hound dog of unknown lineage. He was well-known by most people and dogs in town and possessed an agreeable personality. There were a few dogs, however, that he did

A skiff built by Jake Dennett similar to "The Rowboat."
Photo courtesy of Wilson Museum

not like, and they had learned to keep a good distance away from Obadiah. He was considered by some to be the top dog in town.

The neighborhood was Sunday-morning quiet. No one else was about, no wind ruffled the Bagaduce River, and the sun, just starting to show at the horizon north of Blue Hill, was turning a dark sky to light blue. This was a perfect day for a row.

Neither of the Dennett brothers, Jake and Joe, was at the wharf. It would be another two or three hours before they arrived, but the walkway on the left side of their building provided access to the wharf and floats. The Rowboat, along with several others, was tied to the float by a line attached to her bow. Dave had learned from experience that boarding a small boat over the bow is not a good idea. Stability is close to zero, so the result of this technique can be an unexpected dunk. He untied the line at the float end, pushed the boat out free of the others, then maneuvered her to a location where she could be tied up alongside. Rain from the previous day had left water in the bilge. Dave sat on the gunwale, moving water out from under the floorboards, and commenced to bail with a rusty tin can that was kept along with a sponge under the stern seat. As he was finishing, steps sounded on the gangway behind him, and Obadiah's bark announced someone's arrival.

Raymond Bowden stepped onto the float carrying two clam hods and a rake.

"Well, hello to you, too, Obadiah. You're up early, boy, where you goin'?"

"Haven't decided yet, just going for a row. Maybe Islesboro."

"Islesboro! Why would you want to do that? You shouldn't be out on the Bay in that little boat. Must be a girl you know over there. Is that it?"

"No, I just like to row, and Islesboro's an interesting place. Where are you going clamming?"

"Well, now, I don't generally say. That's a trade secret, you know. Fishermen don't say where they catch fish, and clammers don't say where they get clams. But I suppose you could just follow me to find out. I think I'll try Ram Island. Or if that doesn't work, maybe I'll move over to Indian Bar. Low tide's at eight thirty, so I'm already late, and I'm supposed to be home by noon. Irene's invited some people in for Sunday dinner, and I need to be cleaned up for that. Give me a hand with this boat, will ya?"

Raymond set the two hods down, put the rake inside one of them and moved over to his boat, which was lying upside down on the float. It was a flat-bottom skiff, built a few years ago by Jake with help from his nephew, Dyke; or maybe the other way around, as Dyke had done most of the building. He was only ten years old at the time, but had been working with his uncle for a year or more. The quality of his work was that of someone much older and with years of boatbuilding experience. Dyke was a natural, and Jake had taught him well.

Dave got out of The Rowboat to help Raymond turn the skiff over and slide it into the water. Raymond put his clamming gear in, boarded, pulled the oars out from under the seats, and pushed off from the float.

"Raymond, don't you take anything to eat? It's a long time till dinner."

"Oh, well, I'll eat a few clams."

"You start a fire to cook 'em?"

"No, boy, I eat 'em raw. They're best that way, you know. Have you never had raw clams?"

"I always eat 'em steamed or fried."

"Well, you should try 'em raw. I've heard they make ya horny, although at my age it doesn't seem to work... and at your age you prob'ly don't need 'em. You take care out on the Bay. It's gonna be a hot day, so there'll be a sea breeze this afternoon. Make sure you're back before that happens." Raymond put his back to the oars, but then paused and looked over at Dave again. "Not a good idea to be out on the Bay in that little boat. Does your mother know you're goin'?"

Dave shook his head and put his lunch bag and canteen under the forward seat. Obadiah jumped in and settled himself in the stern seat. Dave boarded and started to row; past the town dock, around the Academy ship, *American Sailor*, and finally in the direction of the bell buoy. Raymond, just ahead of him, was rowing toward the monument, a cut-granite structure that marked a ledge near the Brooksville shore. He was probably in hopes of getting across the Nautilus Island bar before the tide was too low. It looked like he might have to drag the boat a short distance, as much of the bar was showing. Dave changed direction with the thought of helping, but there turned out to be sufficient water near the middle of the bar. Raymond made it across and continued toward Ram Island.

Dave reset his course for the bell buoy, pulling hard on the oars. The only sounds were creaks from the oar locks with each stroke and water tumbling alongside at the bow. Obadiah lay on the stern seat with his chin resting on the port gunwale, happy to be included in the day's outing. Dave continued past the buoy in a westerly direction and, with no wind and only a slight current to oppose his progress, made an easy row to the Pripet area of Islesboro. He then turned north, following the shore around Turtle Head to a cove where he beached the boat.

Obadiah jumped from the stern seat, landed in the water, and ran up the beach. He found an abundance of driftwood on which to lift his leg. Dave pulled the boat up so she was partially out of the water, set the small anchor behind a rock, then retrieved his lunch and canteen from the bow. He noted that it was eight thirty, so the tide was just about low and would start flooding soon. He was ready to rest his arms, and Obadiah seemed to want some action, so the two of them set off for a walk through the woods. They found the path that led to the end of Turtle Head, but rather than go in that direction, Dave chose to turn right. A fifteen-minute walk brought them to Islesboro's main road which went the entire length of the island and made a loop at the north end. It was this loop that the path led to. Obadiah, always in the lead, turned to look at Dave. Which direction? But Dave called him back to return along the path. He was not comfortable leaving the boat on the beach with the tide now coming in.

Dave spent the next hour poking though the driftwood and flotsam, eating one of his sandwiches, and finally resting on the sand with his back against a large log. As Raymond had predicted, it was turning into a hot day even on this island surrounded by fifty-five degree water. There probably will be a good sea breeze and resulting waves, so it would be best to get back to Castine before one o'clock. He looked at his pocket watch: five past ten. He should leave by ten thirty. Obadiah, having eaten one of the dog biscuits, was stretched out on the sand, seemingly asleep in the sun. Dave found a comfortable position. His early morning start was catching up with him, and the warm sun felt good. It was not long before he, too, was asleep.

The sound of a horn woke Dave. At first he couldn't think of where he was. He sat up and looked around. The sound had apparently come from a small tug boat a short distance from shore and moving slowly north up Penobscot Bay. It was towing two barges loaded with pulp wood. Dave looked at his watch: ten forty-five. A bit late to start back, so he would row a bit faster. The more immediate problem was the rowboat, now fully afloat and the anchor under water. Dave took his shoes and socks off, rolled up his pant legs, waded in to retrieve the anchor, and pulled the boat back to shore. The water was cold and deeper than he had estimated. His pants were not rolled up far enough.

With Obadiah, shoes and food back on board, Dave pushed the boat off the beach and climbed in over the side. As he started rowing north along the shoreline, he looked over to his right at the tug and barges. The tug looked to be about fifty feet long, made of steel as evidenced by a few rusty streaks on the black hull and newly painted white topsides. They were moving very slowly, even slower than the rowboat. An American flag flew at the top of its mast, and a Canadian flag hung from a halyard below it. Dave's curiosity moved him to change course so that he would intercept the tug and perhaps find out where she was from. New Brunswick probably, bringing pulp wood to the Bucksport paper mill. He noticed a small building occupying an open space on the forward end of the first barge, and two people sitting on a bench next to it. They waved, and Dave responded by holding up his right hand, still grasping the oar, and giving a sort-of wave back. Soon he had the rowboat alongside the barge and moving at the same speed. A woman, about Dave's mother's age, said hello, and the girl next to her, about Dave's age, smiled at him. It was a beautiful smile as was everything else about her. Light brown hair fell to her shoulders, and a lovely face, tanned from perhaps spending a summer on the water, radiated a personality that Dave immediately wanted to know. She had blue eyes and was not very tall. A pair of Levi's and pink T-shirt covered, but at the same time showed, her slim figure. Five foot two, eyes of blue, oh, what those eyes do to you. The words from an old song tumbled into the front of his mind from some obscure recess.

"Hello. Where are you from?" Dave asked.

The woman replied, "Oh, we live in Yarmouth... Nova Scotia that is, not Maine, but spend most of the summer here on this rig traveling with my husband. We haul cargo all over the Bay of Fundy. Want to come aboard for a cuppa?"

After an explanation that "cuppa" meant "cup of tea," Dave agreed. He threw his bow line. The girl caught it and made it fast to a deck cleat with a quick series of figure eights. A row of fenders on the side of the barge provided protection for the rowboat, and Dave climbed up to the deck. Obadiah stayed in the stern seat, looking up with only mild interest.

The woman set her mug down on the bench. "I'll get your tea. Would you like a biscuit to go with it? I made 'em this morning."

Dave nodded. "Yes, please. That would be nice."

"Doreen, pull that other bench around so this young man

has a place to sit. Well, now you know my daughter's name is Doreen. Some people call her Dory, but she's not fond of that. Doreen works better. What's your name?"

"David, but Dave works."

"Welcome aboard, David. My name's Margaret, not Maggie, not Marge—it's Margaret. I'll get your tea and biscuit." She ducked in under the low door to the building just as Doreen came around the side carrying a wooden stool.

"The bench is kinda heavy; I hope this is okay."

The two sat down, Dave on the stool facing and near one end of the bench, Doreen on the far end, which left the middle seat for Margaret. Doreen looked at Dave, smiled and obviously expected him to start a conversation. He, flustered, blurted out, "Do you ever row?", then thought to himself, "What a stupid thing to say!" But Doreen apparently didn't think so.

"Yes, I like to row. We carry a skiff on *Queen Bea*." She pointed at the tug boat. Large letters on the stern showed that name plus YARMOUTH N.S. Dave could also see a lapstrake boat lying upside down on the after deck's hatch cover. Doreen continued, "We use that to get ashore when we're moored for the night—you know, to get groceries, or walk around town, or, if there's a theatre, go to the movies. If there's nothing going on ashore, I sometimes drop Mom and Dad off here and row by myself, just to explore."

Dave marveled that she was spending the summer on the water and was just a bit envious. "Where did the name *Queen Bea* come from?"

"My grandmother's name was Beatrice, and she had kind of a strong personality. Liked to be in charge. Dad named the tug for her. It was sort of a family joke, but Gramma was pleased, so the name stayed. Dad's like her. He likes to be in charge, too."

Margaret appeared with a steaming mug and a plate with several cookies. Dave got up as she passed the mug and plate to him. He had expected biscuits, the kind Mom baked to go with beans on Saturday night. These "biscuits" were cake-like, chocolate, and with sugar sprinkled on top. The situation Dave found himself in was getting better with each passing minute: a beautiful day on the water, sitting and talking with a gorgeous girl, and biscuits were now chocolate cookies.

The three of them sat, Dave facing the other two. He sipped his tea. It was very hot. He let it drain to the bottom of his mouth, then breathed in and out several times in an attempt to cool it before swallowing. Doreen watched with an amused look. As Dave bit into his biscuit (it was delicious), Margaret spoke.

"Now, David, tell us about yourself. Where do you live and what do you do? Are you in school? High school? College?"

Dave pointed off to the starboard side and said he lived over there in the town of Castine. "I'll be a senior in high school this fall and plan to go to college next year. I like science and plan to major in physics. I've got a job this summer at the golf course, mainly mowing grass with a tractor. It's not very exciting, but I get a pay check every Saturday."

"Have you got brothers and sisters?"

"Two older sisters and a younger brother. My father teaches at Maine Maritime Academy, and my mother runs the Castine Coal Company in addition to running the house."

"Doreen's coming up on senior year in high school, too. Then what, Doreen?"

"I plan to go to Dalhousie University in Halifax. My grades are good enough that I'm pretty sure they'll take me. I'll major in education, but want to be a science teacher, so I'll take as many of those courses as I can, especially biology."

Dave finished eating the first biscuit, then said, "Did you know there's a connection between Castine and Dalhousie?"

Doreen shook her head.

Dave continued, "Castine was occupied by British troops during the War of 1812, and all of the fees collected at the customs house were put toward an endowment for Dalhousie. At least that's what one of the historic signs in town says."

"Maybe you'd like to go to Dalhousie to study physics. They might give you a special scholarship as you come from Castine."

Dave wasn't sure if Doreen was joking, but the idea of going to the same college as she appealed to him. The conversation continued, and when tea and biscuits were finished Dave realized that they had passed Stockton Harbor and were coming up on Cape Jellison. It would be a long row against the tide and wind to get back home, so Dave explained that he had to be on his way and thanked Margaret for her hospitality. He turned to Doreen.

"I'd like to see you again. I could come to Bucksport if you're going to be there for a while. Maybe we could go to supper tonight. Crosby's is a neat take-out place."

"I'd like to, but I don't think that can work. We're just there to unload wood this afternoon, then leave as soon as possible. We're supposed to be at Grand Manan Tuesday morning. And we're not supposed to even go ashore in Bucksport. U.S. customs people don't like that. But I'm glad we met, and maybe we'll both be at Dalhousie next year. Think about it."

Obadiah banged his tail on the seat in greeting as Dave climbed down into the rowboat. The dog, at least, was glad to be on the way home. As Dave set his oars and reluctantly pulled away from the barge, Doreen called out. "Will you write to me?"

"Yes! What's your address?"

"17 Pleasant Street, Yarmouth."

Dave thought, "I can remember that, we're both *seventeen* years old, and this was the most *pleasant* day I've had in a long time."

The Halls' Night Out

"Gol durn this car." Mr. Hall expressed his most vehement cuss words in exasperation with the 1940 Chevrolet sedan. He had driven to the post office this afternoon for the mail, and nothing was wrong then. But now, even after pumping the accelerator and nearly standing on the starter pedal, the engine was refusing to go. It had caught momentarily on the first try, then sputtered to silence. The only sound since was of the starter motor.

Mrs. Hall, who was just settling into the passenger seat beside him, turned to look at her husband of forty years. "Now, Mr. Hall, don't get upset. Maybe if you just let it rest for a few minutes it will be ready to go. And if it doesn't, then our ride tonight was just not meant to be."

William and Letitia Hall lived in the gray house at the top of the hill behind Fort George. To William, she was Mrs. Hall, and to Letitia, he was Mr. Hall. She had spent her adult life keeping house, raising their three children, and volunteering at church and other local organizations. He pursued his career in education; a teacher in small rural Maine schools at the beginning, then a faculty member at the Eastern State Normal School in Castine, and finally the principal there. He had retired five years previous, in 1942, when austerity measures, faced by the state legislature, resulted in closing the normal school.

"The car doesn't get tired. It either starts or it doesn't start, and if it doesn't, there's something wrong that needs to be fixed." Mr. Hall's irritation was still showing, while Mrs. Hall was moving on to thoughts on how to solve the problem.

"The last time it wouldn't go, Horace Leach came and did something to the engine. It only took him a minute and then it started right up. Did you see what he did? Could you try that?" Things mechanical were complete mysteries to Mrs. Hall, but she had full, if misplaced, confidence in her husband.

"I did watch. Horace said the choke was stuck closed, and that was flooding the carburetor. He wiggled some rods on top of the engine and oiled them. I guess I could try wiggling them." Mr. Hall got out of the car, lifted the hood, and peered in. Somehow it did not look the same as when Horace was here, but there were some rods and thingies near a round something-or-other that he thought was the entrance for air. He reached for one of the rods, and just as he touched it, it snapped forward. "Hmm. Maybe that was it. But if it is flooded I should wait a few minutes."

Soon after, when Mr. Hall stepped on the starter pedal, the engine came to life accompanied by Mrs. Hall's words of admiration. He backed out of the driveway and drove down the hill toward the old normal school classroom building that was now occupied by Maine Maritime Academy. Seeing these buildings always brought a pang of sadness—sadness that the Normal School, after seventy-five years of student teachers in attendance, was gone—and regret that he had not been able to save it. He missed the camaraderie of faculty members, and he missed the classroom filled with mostly eager students. But the campus was being well used by the Academy, and graduates had played important parts in the war effort, both naval and merchant service.

He slowed near the bottom of the hill, as cars were parked at the side of the road. Out of the corner of his eye, he could see that several people were walking across the field toward Fort George. They must be going to the final rehearsal of the Castine Pageant, a play that was being held in the Fort this year rather than on the Emerson Hall stage. Mr. Hall and Margaret Ames had been instrumental in organizing the production last year.

He stopped the Chevrolet at the intersection of Backshore Road and Battle Avenue. "Which way, Mrs. Hall? Do you want to go just around the town, or shall we go all the way around the square?" "The square" was a road loop that went from "one-mile corner" along Route 166 to "six-mile corner" and back to the start via Route 166A. As the names imply, the start was about one mile from town and the loop was about ten miles long. At the leisurely speed that Mr. Hall drove, it would take a half hour to complete the trip.

Mrs. Hall hesitated only slightly before replying, "Let's go around the square, and come home by the Backshore Road."

"You don't think that's tempting fate, do you? Remember our car didn't want us to go anywhere tonight."

Mrs. Hall just smiled at him, and Mr. Hall turned left onto Battle Avenue. It was a mostly uneventful ride. They stopped at Dunk's Meadow hoping to see the snowy egret that had been sighted there a few days previous, but the only water birds visible were two mallards swimming into the reeds. Just past the Methodist Chapel they paused to watch three deer in the field, perhaps a mother and her two fawns. She stood quietly while the youngsters romped and played. As they returned to town Mr. Hall took the right that took them past the backshore and swimming pool, past Don Hutchins' house and then up the hill toward home. As they approached Grace Neely's Hump, a short steep portion of the road with level stretches on both sides, an oncoming car on the upper level section appeared then momentarily disappeared as the Halls' car reached the bottom of the Hump. A sudden feeling of unease came over Mr. Hall.

Eddie Talbert was from Jersey City. Born there, he had spent most of his twenty-seven years in that area. He was not a big man, barely five-feet-six and weighing one hundred-twenty pounds, but he had a handsome face, reddish blond hair, and an engaging smile. He made friends easily. After struggling through high school academics he had worked in restaurants bussing tables. More recently, it was taxi-driving, but last fall he had landed a job as chauffeur for the Harold Cavanaugh family. Their home was on Fifth Avenue overlooking Central Park. It was a home like Eddie had never seen before: large rooms, beautiful furniture, oil paintings on the walls, and a cook and maid to run the house. The family spent a portion of the winter season in Miami, with Mr. Cavanaugh traveling by train back to New York periodically to keep up with his business pursuits. This summer they were renting a house in Castine for the month of August. Eddie went wherever they went, and he was having a great time. The pay was good, he had his own room, meals were provided in the kitchen with the cook and maid, and he seldom worked more than five hours a day.

When Eddie started his job, Mr. Cavanaugh's vehicle was a 1935 Packard Standard Eight, considered by many to be the ultimate American luxury car of The Thirties. The exterior was a light gray lower body with dark gray for the upper portion, fenders, and running boards. The grill and bumpers were chrome as were the headlight and parking light enclosures mounted atop the front fenders. The spare tire was located beside the hood on the driver's side with the lower part of the tire in a shallow fender well. The tires were mounted on wire wheels sporting small chrome hubcaps with bright red insignias at the center. There was no "trunk" built into the body; rather a folding rack above the rear bumper held a real trunk. Although eleven years old, the Packard was still an impressive car: luxurious for passengers and a fine example of prewar automotive design and craftsmanship. It still turned the heads of many who saw it.

Eddie loved the car and he loved driving it. He spent hours nearly every day cleaning inside and out: vacuuming the wool carpets, polishing the wood interior trim, and applying softening liquid to the leather seats. The outside was dusted or washed if any mud showed. A Simonize job was in order once every month. He even crawled under the car to remove mud and other debris from the undercarriage. He was not allowed to do mechanical work on the Packard, but read and reread the maintenance manual to understand every system. He added several items to the tool kit that came with the car. If something were to fail on a lonely highway, Eddie felt that he would be able to fix it.

One day in April while driving Mr. Cavanaugh to his office, Eddie was instructed to take the Packard to a certain car dealer in lower Manhattan. The Packard was being traded for a new Cadillac that would be ready for delivery that afternoon. Eddie was stunned, but tried not to show it. After all, how could one have feelings of affection for anything mechanical? Well, he did, and he spent the rest of the morning with the Packard: washing and waxing the outside, cleaning the inside, and applying special leather treatment to the seats. After lunch he drove slowly down Fifth Avenue, turned onto Eleventh Street and parked under the Cadillac sign. It felt like driving in a funeral procession. Eddie removed the key from the ignition, locked the doors, and ran his hand across the top of the hood. He hoped the Packard would find a good home with someone who appreciated the fine automobile that it was.

The new car was not bad; a Series Sixty Special Fleetwood, black exterior, tan cloth interior, a V8 engine and automatic transmission. Eddie had never driven a car with the latter, and he was not impressed. His choice would be to do his own shifting rather than some gremlin under his feet doing it. Automatic transmissions were for people who were too lazy to work the clutch and choose the gear. The seats were spacious and comfortable, the car accelerated faster than the Packard, and the salesman told Eddie that it had a one hundred-fifty horsepower engine and a top speed of a hundred miles an hour. Eddie was interested in that last number, but couldn't think of any road where he could try for it—maybe on the way to Florida next winter. No, the Cavanaughs would be in the back seat and never go for that. It would have to be sometime when he had the car by himself.

Castine was a complete mystery to Eddie. He had never been north of Hartford before this summer, and had never been in a small village for more time than it takes to buy gasoline or lunch. Whenever he went downtown, complete strangers would say hello. Eddie didn't know what to do. Were they setting him up for some sort of game? To take advantage? And driving. Quite often a driver coming in the opposite direction, one hand on top of the wheel, would lift a finger just as the cars were about to pass. At first Eddie was miffed, thinking it an insult, but then he realized it was always the index finger. What was that about? Must be some sort of signal, maybe there was a cop ahead. But he never saw any cops. Lewis, the mechanic at Leach's Chevrolet Garage, told him there was only one state trooper in the area, "Trooper Rupert," and he seldom came to Castine. Eddie started lifting his index finger, too.

There didn't seem to be much to do for excitement here. The summer people spent time playing golf or tennis, going out in boats, and attending cocktail parties. The locals worked during the day and disappeared by late afternoon. Eddie liked to go out drinking with his buddies back home, but he didn't know anyone here and there was no bar in town. Macomber's Grocery Store did sell beer. Eddie went there once a week to buy a few bottles of Narragansett, but it was not very exciting to drink beer by himself. Liza, the Cavanaughs' maid, was about Eddie's age and quite attractive. However, she had a boyfriend back in New York and had never shown interest in Eddie. But now, far from New York and that boyfriend, she was showing symptoms of "out of sight, out of mind" and displaying more interest in Eddie with each passing day. He saw an opportunity there, and this morning, at breakfast, she had agreed to go with him in the Cadillac to watch the sunset at the backshore.

Sydney Greenbie and John Pratt stood near the south entrance to Fort George. They were continuing their somewhat animated discussion of the previous evening on production costs for

The cast of "The Pageant," Castine's dramatized biography of a town, circa 1948. The author is seated third from right in the front row, wearing a feather head dress. Photo courtesy of Castine Historical Society

the Castine Pageant. More had been spent on costumes, scenery, and advertising than the sum of their treasury plus expected ticket sales. Where was the balance coming from? Tempers had cooled somewhat overnight, and they both came to understand that a compromise was close: one that would be good for the Pageant and that would not damage egos. They shook hands, and moved toward the stage where the first act was about to start.

The Pageant, written by Sydney and Marjorie Greenbie, was, in their words, "a dramatized biography of a town," covering the time period of the first recorded visit of Europeans to this area, 1604, to the end of World War II, 1945. It was first produced on the Emerson Hall stage in the summer of 1946 as part of the sesquicentennial of Castine's incorporation as a town. It was repeated several times in the following years. One of the presentations was at Fort George on a stage built in the east corner rampart.

On this August night, as the Halls' car approached Grace

Neely's Hump, the Pageant's dress rehearsal was taking place at the Fort. John Pratt played the part of Jean Vincent, Baron de Saint Castin, a French nobleman of the seventeenth century. He wore an appropriate costume: flowing black jacket, black trousers tucked inside black boots and a wide-brimmed black hat with a large white feather waving from one side. He was an imposing sight. Janet Guild was the beautiful Matilda, daughter of the local Indian chief, Madockawanda, and wife of the Baron. John Gray, as Miles Standish, wore a military uniform complete with metal breast plate and helmet. Others played the parts of fur trappers, clergymen, early settlers and soldiers. The play was directed by Charlene Devereux who insisted on costumes that were both historically accurate and visually impressive.

A half hour after Sydney's and John's conversation, the first act was in progress. Charles Hodgkins, playing the part of Samuel de Champlain, was speaking.

"Wonderful, wonderful, rich and beautiful beyond all the lands that God has given man. But how am I to find means to make discoveries in this New France for the profit and glory of the French name? How am I to lead these poor natives to God, and protect them from the merciless greed of our fur traders? How can I persuade men in France to leave their hovels and begin life again, fresh and clean, in this Garden of Eden?"

As Charles turned dramatically to look to his right, supposedly toward the river, a horrendous crash of metal against metal came from beyond the west corner of the fort. All rehearsal activities stopped, and everyone, as if on command, started running in that direction. They went up and over the fort's ramparts and across the dry moat. When they reached the road and looked down toward Grace Neely's Hump, a Chevrolet sedan was at the side of the road. It was not moving. Steam rose from under the hood, and the driver's side of the car was thoroughly smashed. Farther down the hill and off the road to the right, the side of a black Cadillac was visible, its front end embracing a large oak tree. The troupe of players continued rapidly down the hill toward the two wrecked cars.

Mr. Hall, dazed, could not understand what had happened, and blood covered his right hand. Where did that come from? He looked at his wife. She was slumped sideways with her head resting against the door frame, and blood flowed from a gash on her jaw. "Letitia, Letitia! Are you all right?"

She moaned softly and moved her head to look at him. "Oh, Mr. Hall, your forehead's bleeding, and there's blood on my dress; oh no, it's on the seat cover, too."

"Don't worry about the seat cover. You've got a bad cut on your jaw." He reached over to touch her face. "Here, let me help. I've got a clean handkerchief." He pulled it from his pocket and gently pushed it against her face to stop the flow of blood.

Mrs. Hall winced at the touch, then asked, "What happened? It was all so fast, I don't understand."

"When we came over the crest of the hill, that other car was right there, coming at us, fast. I guess they swerved at the last moment because it's only this side of our car that got hit. Maybe I should go see if the people in the other car are all right... No, we need to get you to the hospital."

Mr. Hall's mind was racing through countless thoughts but with no focus on any one. He sat back for a moment, took a deep breath, and then put Mrs. Hall's hand on the handkerchief to hold it against her jaw. He stepped on the starter pedal. Nothing happened. He pushed again, still nothing. Pulling on the door handle and pushing against the door with his shoulder produced only pain in the latter. The door was jammed shut.

"What do we do now?" she asked. "Oh, there are some people coming, lots of them. Who are they?" A short distance in front of the car, a crowd of people was hurrying down the road toward them. "They'll help us."

Mr. Hall looked up from the speedometer that had become the object of his intense study. "I don't know who they are. Look how they're dressed, old fashioned clothes." A disturbing thought suddenly entered his mind. "Mrs. Hall… do you suppose that we are dead, and these are the spirits of people we've known come to greet us?"

By now, some in the crowd had arrived at the car, and were peering in through the windows. Faces looked vaguely familiar, but their coloring was odd and their clothing was completely strange. Here was a Catholic priest in his long black robe looking in the window and saying, "Mrs. Hall, don't worry, you're going to be okay." Did this mean that medical help was on the way? Or did it mean that all of the Halls' earthly cares were behind them, that they were now in heaven? But they weren't Catholics. Why wouldn't it be a Congregational minister to greet them?

Mr. Hall called out, "Father, are we dead? Is this heaven?"

The priest looked at him with a puzzled expression and replied, "You'll be fine, Mr. Hall, there's nothing to worry about."

Mrs. Hall thought that the priest looked a bit like Kenneth Walker, but that didn't make sense. Kenneth was a minister, not a priest. Her attention suddenly shifted to an Indian woman who was standing in front of the car. "Why, she's not an Indian, that's Lorna Clement, and she's not dead. I saw her when I went to the library this morning. She's fine. She was walking their dog, Penney. Oh… all of these people are in the Pageant, that's why they're dressed so funny. We're not dead, Mr. Hall."

Later that evening Mr. and Mrs. Hall and Liza, the Cavanaughs' maid, were in the Castine Hospital having been taken there in the back seat of Dr. Babcock's Plymouth station wagon. Therma Douglas, a nurse at the hospital, was in the play as a 1771 Castine settler, so had been there to assist the doctor at the accident scene. She rode to the hospital in the front seat. The Halls' injuries were not serious, but the doctor kept them there overnight, checked them over again in the morning, and they were back home by dinnertime. They both had painful bumps and bruises, and it was more than a month before they were completely recovered. Their experience of "Are we dead or not?" was a topic of family discussion for many years after.

Liza suffered a concussion, a broken wrist, and several broken ribs. She was in the hospital for two days, and when released, was not able to perform the duties expected of a maid. The Cavanaughs sent her back to New York to be cared for by her family, and she resumed her maid's job with them in September. She never saw or spoke to Eddie again.

The Cadillac, with just 1,537 miles on the odometer, and the Chevrolet were both total wrecks. They were towed to Rolnick's Auto Salvage in Veazie and dismantled, the parts eventually being reused in other 1947 Cadillacs and 1940 Chevrolets.

Eddie was not seriously hurt in the accident, and since there was no room for him in Dr. Babcock's car, John Hoctor, the Academy football coach, gave him a ride. John was dressed as another seventeenth century French nobleman, Charles D'Aulnay. At the hospital Beulla Rowell, the head nurse, checked Eddie over. Other than a bruise and slight cut on his chin, he was fine. The next morning a taxi arrived at the Cavanaughs' rental house and transported Eddie to Union Station in Bangor. He rode the train back to New York. Later that fall, a rumor surfaced in Castine that Eddie was driving a taxi in Brooklyn, New York.

Orrin's Rescue

Orrin walked across the gravel parking lot toward the town wharf and paused in front of Gene Bowden's hot-dog stand. Gene had been there earlier in the morning readying it for opening next week, but had left to make the afternoon mail run to Bucksport. Orrin liked Gene's hamburgers and fried onion rings, but they were a treat he could seldom afford. He continued to the outer end of the wharf and sat on a bench in the sun facing the water. It was early June and this was the first day that truly felt like summer. There had been teasing days in May, even late April, when the back door thermometer approached seventy, but they had each ended with a cold northwest wind that discouraged all but grass and crocuses. Orrin had spent the morning readying the public toilet building at the town waterfront area for the summer, a job normally done by Charlie Thayer. Charlie was at the veterans hospital recovering from surgery and would not be able to return to the waterfront job for several more weeks, so Orrin was filling in. He had swept cobwebs from corners and washed the fixtures, walls, and floors. He'd come back later after the floors dried and paint them. It was good to have the chance to earn a few extra dollars, but he would not choose this job if anything else was available.

Orrin opened his dinner box and took out a can of sardines, a paper bag containing Saltine Crackers, and a thermos bottle. The waterfront area was deserted save for Victor Black's lobster boat which was tied up at the end of the wharf and visible only because the tide was high. As he started his meager meal, his mind turned to a self-appraisal. It happened occasionally, this voice inside. He did not like it. He tried to put it away, to think of something else, but somehow it persisted. It lectured to him.

Orrin, you're wasting your life. You're forty years old, you're living at home with your elderly parents, you're not taking care of your children, and you're not accomplishing a thing that's of any use. God gave you more than your fair share of talents. You graduated from high school with honor grades, and you were a star player in both basketball and baseball. You even had a successful year at the Normal School. You need to do something with those talents.

Orrin turned these thoughts over in his mind, and then replied to himself, "I do accomplish some things. I take care of Mom and Dad, do things around the house that they can't do any more. I've got three part-time jobs, and half of the money earned I give to Sally and the kids. And when the kids come to spend the night with me and the folks I help them with their homework and read bedtime stories to them. Oh, and I help coach the high school baseball team. And I always go to their plays and basketball games. I do a lot."

But it's not enough, is it, Orrin? Three part-time jobs? They only add up to ten or fifteen dollars a week. What is it that prevents you from being a real father? What broke up your marriage? Why did you get fired from that job at the mill? You still love Sally, and that was a good job, but. But what, Orrin?

"I've just had bad luck, it's not my fault."

It's not bad luck, Orrin, and you know that. Come on, come clean with yourself. It's the bottle, Orrin. It's the bottle. That's what broke up your marriage, the reason you can't be a real father, and that's why you lost the mill job. You need to admit that and do something about it. There are people in town who have offered to help, and you've been too proud to accept. You think you can do it on your own, but you can't. Get some help, Orrin. You've still got plenty of time to make a good life for yourself, to be a man your children can be proud of.

Orrin ate the last bit of sardine and poured the remaining oil from the can over a Saltine cracker to finish his meal. He washed it down with water from the thermos and put the tin can, crumpled paper bag and thermos back inside the dinner box. He leaned back against the single board at the top of the bench thinking that perhaps the voice in his head was finished for now, and that he could relax in the sun while waiting for the floors to dry. The voice was finished, but the message was still there. He thought about asking Willie Clark for help. Willie was a part-time preacher and had offered to help last year. Orrin went on to think about what he might find for a real job. "Maybe one at the Academy. They're always looking for painters and carpenters, and I'm reasonably good at both. The dream job, though, is to work with the athletic teams, maybe an assistant coach. Would that be possible? Maybe I can talk with Harry Small, my old high school principal. He teaches there now."

"Orrin? The women's bathroom is locked up, and we'd like to use it. Have you got a key? Can you open it for us?"

Orrin turned. Two high school girls stood at the edge of the parking lot looking across the wharf at him. They each carried a

Castine town dock, circa 1938. The small white building is the public toilet building Orrin painted. The brick building at right is Wardwell's Market.
Photo courtesy of Castine Historical Society

paper bag. "The bathroom's not workin' yet, water's not turned on."

"That doesn't matter. All we want to do is change into bathing suits." They held up the bags.

"Oh. Well, I guess that's all right, but I washed the floor this morning, and I'm about to paint. You can't get any dirt on it."

"We won't. We'll take our shoes off and go in barefoot."

Orrin got up and walked across the wharf. "Why aren't you in school? School's not out yet, is it?" ("Who are these girls?" he thought. "Familiar faces, but I can't think of their names.")

One of them replied. "No, school's not out yet, but we, ah..."

The other girl continued. "They let the senior honor students out for the afternoon, and everybody else is getting remedial help. We're both seniors on the honor roll."

Orrin grunted and thought, "I bet they're playing hooky," but continued toward the small white building housing the bathrooms. He opened the women's side and checked the floor. It was dry. "Remember, don't track any dirt in there."

The girls nodded, toed their shoes off on the outside step

and went in, closing the door behind them. Orrin went around to the men's bathroom door, opened it, and removed the can of paint from the shelf above the sink. "Might as well get started." He took the paint to the outside step, opened it and began stirring. A few minutes later the girls walked by wearing bathing suits and carrying towels. "Swimming now?" Orrin remembered that was the sort of thing he might have done twenty-five years ago, but the thought of jumping into Bagaduce River water, especially this early in the summer, had no appeal at all. It made him shiver just to think of it. He finished stirring and reached into the box of rags Mack Wardwell had given him. Mack said there was a paint brush there. Orrin found one, but it was hard with dried paint and unusable. He pondered this for a minute, then mumbled to himself, "Guess I'll have to go up to the hardware store and get a new one. Hope George will let me charge it to the town. He will if I tell him about Charlie being over at Togus and I'm fillin' in."

Part of what Betty and Judith told Orrin was true. They were both seniors, very good students, consistently on the honor roll, and were in the midst of a friendly competition for valedictorian, but Orrin had been correct in thinking that they were playing hooky. Graduation was a week away, and final exams were in progress. They had taken their chemistry test that morning, and the schedule for the afternoon included review sessions in history and English. Both felt confident of A-grades in those courses. Neither Betty nor Judith had ever skipped school, something the two of them had talked about several days before. They decided that their high school experience would not be complete without doing that at least once, so made plans for the next good day; plans to either walk in Witherle Woods or, if warm enough, swim off the town wharf. Today was that day, and it was warm. After lunch, and before the one o'clock bell rang, they met in the girls bathroom, each carrying a paper bag containing a bathing suit and towel. They went upstairs, through the science lab, and down the enclosed fire escape on the back of the school building. Coming out through the lower door, they found classmates Jay Pratt and Dick Harman sharing a cigarette. That was completely against the rules.

"We're goin' to tell on you," Judith piped up.

Jay looked up. "And I guess we'll tell on you. It looks like you're playin' hooky. That's the reason you're sneakin' out the fire escape 'stead of using the front door. Mr. Calkins is gonna be some surprised to find out his two goody-goody girls are bein' bad."

"Oh... How about we won't tell on you if you don't tell on us, although I guess Mr. Calkins will find out about us anyway."

"Okay, have fun."

The girls left, going behind the barn of the house next door and walking rapidly across George Faye's lawn toward Court Street. Rather than following a direct route to the waterfront, they turned left, then down Dyers Lane and along Water Street to the downtown area. They saw only two people on the way. The first was Jute Mixer who came out of his house and walked along the street in front of them. He paid no attention to two delinquent high school students. The second person was a potential problem, Spunk Hatch, the truant officer. He came out of the drugstore as Judith and Betty passed the movie theater, but didn't see them as they slipped behind the corner of Leach's Garage. They waited for the sound of his truck engine to fade, then proceeded to the waterfront area using the stairs between the telephone office and the brick building.

A short time later they were changed into their suits and sitting at the edge of the float, stretching legs down to get toes into the frigid water and working on enough courage to jump in.

"I don't think I can do this."

"But we've talked about it for days. If we don't go in, our whole afternoon of skipping school will be wasted. Come on. We'll just jump in and get right out, then lie here on the float in the sun. It'll feel really good. Remember that bit in *Moby-Dick* about Ishmael sleeping in that cold room at the Spouter Inn? The contrast between cozy warm and frigid cold? It makes the cozy warm feel all the better. The heat of the sun will be like that."

With that, they jumped off the float into the Bagaduce River. Betty led, leaping off with arms spread wide. She hit feet-first, the water enveloping her, seeming to pull her below the surface, farther than expected. It was shockingly cold and at first none of

The Castine waterfront, circa 1955, with the town wharf at the center of the photograph. Photo courtesy of Castine Historical Society

her muscles responded, but then feet kicked and her face broke through to air. Judith had just hit the water, and moments later the two of them were laughing with excitement.

"Let's get out of this. It's cold."

As they turned to swim toward the ladder to the wharf, Victor's boat was square in their vision. It was tied up against the wharf and blocked the ladder, their intended way out.

"We should have looked at that before we jumped in. What do we do now?"

"Let's try getting up on the float."

They swam to that possible way out of the problem, and they could reach up far enough to grab the edge, but didn't have strength enough to pull themselves up.

"Where's the closest beach? Someplace we can swim to and walk out."

They looked in both directions at the Castine waterfront, and saw only water lapping on wharves and bulkheads, no place in sight for swimmers to get out of the water.

"There's that sandy one over the other side of the Academy wharf, and there's one between Dennett's and Mace Eaton's, but I don't know if I can swim that far."

"There must be someone who can help us... HELP! Someone help!" Betty felt the cold water sapping strength from her muscles, and calling out seemed the only thing left.

"Orrin was there, but he was going inside the to paint the floor. He'll never hear us. Oh, God, what are we gonna do? I don't want to die!"

Orrin had started up the hill toward George Coombs' hardware store when a troubling thought came to mind. "I wonder if those girls are okay. Maybe I should check on 'em." He turned around, walking rapidly toward the wharf, and as he got close heard panicky voices calling for help. He ran down the ramp and arrived at the edge of the float to find two terrified faces staring up. Orrin knelt and reached his right hand down to the closest girl.

"Grab my wrist and I'll grab yours. That'll give a good solid grip." Betty did as she was told, and suddenly felt herself yanked from the water and up over the edge of the float. Orrin set her down where she lay on her stomach gasping for breath. Judith was pulled from the water in a similar way.

The girls turned down Orrin's suggestion that he go up to Wardwell's Market to use a phone and call their parents to come get them. They didn't want anyone to know about their skipping school, especially parents. They dried off and went back to the women's bathroom to change into their clothes, hoping to get to school in time to catch the bus home. They thanked Orrin profusely and asked him not to tell anyone. They were soon on their way up Main Street.

Orrin also made his way up Main Street to see George Coombs for a paint brush and a can of brush cleaner. He returned to his painting job and finished the floors late that afternoon. The last thing he did before starting for home was to clean the new brush thoroughly. He would get the leftover paint and brush back to Mack tomorrow, but for now he left them on the shelf over the sink in the men's room. He thought, "I've had six hours of work today, so that's six dollars, pretty good. Wish I could do that every day."

Orrin crossed the parking lot and started up the hill toward home. When he arrived at Water Street, he paused, looking to his right. There was Macomber's Store just a short distance away, and he had enough money with him to buy one bottle of beer. "Why not?" It was more a statement than a question. He turned and started in that direction, but the voice interrupted.

Wait a minute, Orrin. You've done a really good thing this afternoon. Probably no one will ever know about it except those two girls, because they don't want anyone to know they skipped school. And it's just like you to go along with that and not tell anyone. But it was a pretty big thing that you did. You saved their lives. You're a hero. Maybe this is a good time to act like a hero and change your life. Why don't you just turn around and go home?

Orrin stopped walking. He looked along Water Street toward the store, then up Main Street toward home. "Okay, I'll give it a try."

Appendix

Castine Businesses circa 1950

This description of the business community in Castine at mid-twentieth century is an updated version of an article the author wrote for the Castine Historical Society in 2000. It was done with the help of Ruth Dunbar Basile, a classmate at Adams School in the 1940s, and the late Robert Macomber who, except for time at college and in the military, was a life-long resident of the town.

Castine, along with the rest of the country, was still recovering from the effects of the Depression and World War II. Travel by automobile was far less common than now, and local businesses made Castine a more self-sufficient community. In addition to most of the current business types, there were numerous grocery stores, full-service car dealerships, drugstore, hospital, hardware store, barber shop, movie theater, and daily transportation by boat to Belfast.

See the map on pages 186-187.

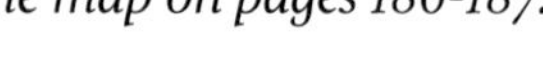

1. Coombs Hardware Store was located at what is now 11 Main Street. (There were no street numbers at that time.) The building was owned by the Masonic Lodge, that group using the upper floors for meetings. George Coombs' store was filled with high shelves that held an amazing variety of items: building, electrical, plumbing and gardening supplies and tools, kitchen equipment, radios and, when television came to Bangor, TV sets.

George repaired electrical appliances and was also a shortwave radio operator with "ham" friends all over the world. He and his wife Edith lived on Green Street. She was the town clerk, tending to those duties from a desk in their home. Their son Merrill produced "The Green Street News" while a student at Adams School. It chronicled the activities and lives of Castine residents along with local business advertisements in the mid-1930s. These newsletters were reissued as a bound volume by Witherle Memorial Library in 1996.

2. Ricker's Variety Store, owned by Willis Ricker and located at 9 Main Street, was a source of newspapers, magazines, candy, office supplies and gifts. Miss Alice Bean worked there as a clerk. Mr. Ricker was a musician, band leader and composer. While a student at the New England Conservatory of Music he played trumpet with the Boston Symphony. In addition to running the store, he sold and tuned pianos, was a member of the Maine State Legislature, and was the town's First Selectman. Several of his musical compositions are on file at the Castine town hall and at the Bagaduce Music Lending Library in Blue Hill. He and his wife lived in the house on the east corner of Court and Pleasant streets.

3. Carl Wardwell Groceries was located at 7 Main Street. Carl was one of several small grocers carrying a limited variety and was in business for many years. He and his wife lived at 10 Perkins Street where she operated a beauty parlor.

4. The IGA Grocery Store was located at 3 Main Street and run by Walter (Bud) Mayo. He carried a full line, including fresh produce and meats. Mrs. Mayo worked in the telephone office. The Kenneth York family from Mars Hill bought the store in the early 1950s, after which Bud was the machine shop instructor at Maine Maritime Academy. The Mayo family lived on Court Street in the house across from the Unitarian Church, the York family on Tarratine Street.

"Ma" Robinson and Maine Maritime Academy students at the counter of the Village Drug Store, circa 1948. Photo courtesy of Castine Historical Society

5. The Village Drug Store was located on the north corner of Main and Water streets and owned by the pharmacist, Walter Robinson. Both Walter and Mrs. Robinson worked in the store, she tending the soda fountain and selling non-prescription items. She was known as "Ma Robinson" by MMA students who came there for coffee and ice cream. In the early 1950s the store was purchased by Edwin Randall who moved here with his family from Tennessee. He was the pharmacist, and Mrs. Randall also worked at the store.

6. Bob Bowden's barbershop was located at 22 Water Street. The Bowdens lived in the family home on the Shore Road near Morse's Cove that was built in the 1700s by Bob's ancestors. Other businesses that were later located there include Poodle's Lobsterette, a restaurant owned by Peter and Scott Vogel's father, and an antique store. The barbershop building was most recently the site

of Fay's One Gallery, but was torn down to be replaced by the present residential building.

7. Leach Brothers Garage, a Chevrolet dealership, was located at 28 Water Street, currently the Berluky building. It was started by brothers Horace and Maxwell Leach, but by 1950 was owned by Horace and his son Willis. Several years later they built a new garage at the top of Windmill Hill, the building currently used by the Brouillard family for several businesses. The Leach garage sold new and used cars, did repair and maintenance work, and sold gasoline.

8. The Folly Theater showed movies on Friday and Saturday evenings. Tickets were eighteen cents for children and twenty-five cents for adults. The building, now gone, was located on Water Street between Leach Brothers Garage and 30 Water Street. It was informally known as "The Tarpaper Palace" and, as that name implies, its demolition was not an architectural tragedy. I believe that the theater was started by Bert Parker and later owned by Horace Leach and George Coombs.

9. Macomber's Store was located across Water Street from the Folly Theater in a building that no longer exists, although concrete foundation walls, visible from Sea Street, may have been part of that building. The store was owned by Austin Macomber who sold a limited supply of groceries and snack items, plus beer. It was the only source of beer in Castine. Tradition holds that Austin had an agreement with Maine Maritime Academy to not sell beer to students. The next nearest store with that beverage was the Hilltop Store in Orland, and there are likely a few older MMA alumni who have memories of occasional trips to Orland.

10. The New England Telephone Company Castine exchange was located in the small white building at 25 Water Street, opposite Bob Bowden's barbershop. The building, still there, is

Margaret Bowden at the switchboard at the New England Telephone Company's Castine exchange.
Photo courtesy of Castine Historical Society

now a residence. Operators were on duty twenty-four hours a day to manually connect callers to their desired numbers. At that time, with no local newspaper, operators were sources of information on what was happening in town. My brother David remembers calling home from college in New York one evening and being told, "Your folks are playing bridge tonight at Buffy and Kath Gray's. I'll connect you to their house." Carrie and Arthur (Tink) Connor, long-time telephone company employees, worked as operators and managed the office. Several other people, including Margaret Bowden and Louise Mayo, were also employed as operators. Edward (Poodle) Vogel did telephone installation and repair work.

11. Marion Clark owned a small grocery store located at 21 Water Street in the brick building on the east corner of Main and Water streets. Mrs. Clark and her husband, Al, previously ran Shattolla House, a summer guest house on Water Street. It consisted of the "Hooke House" plus a series of additions. Lois Moore Cyr has written of this in Castine Historical Society publications.

12. Wardwell's Sanitary Market was located in the "yellow brick building" at the south corner of Main and Water streets. Gus and Algie Wardwell were the proprietors. They carried fruits, vegetables, meats, canned goods, staples and frozen foods. A large walk-in cooler was Gus's domain where meat and other refrigerated goods were kept. He would cut meat and grind hamburger to order at an adjacent wood block counter. Algie usually manned the counter by the cash register and phone. Molasses and vinegar were stored in large wooden barrels with hand pumps that were located in the basement. Customers could bring a container, usually a glass jug, which Gus would take down the steep set of stairs to fill with the desired product. The market also provided home delivery of groceries that could be ordered via phone.

13. Ralph S. Wardwell Real Estate and Insurance was located next to Wardwell's Market in a small building that is now connected to the yellow brick building. Fred Wardwell was the proprietor of this business and ran it with considerable help from the sole employee, Bea Spurling. Oakum Bay Realty is a direct "descendant" of this business.

14. American Sailor Restaurant, in a building that no longer exists, was located on Water Street near what is now the north end of Rogers Hall. It was run by Mrs. McCleod, known as "Ma"

McCleod by MMA students who frequented the restaurant during morning and afternoon coffee breaks. Seating for customers included a counter, behind which food was prepared, and several booths. Pinball machines provided entertainment. Ma's husband ran the food service operation at MMA.

15. Ethel Noyes had a small store located on Water Street to the right of American Sailor Restaurant in another building that was torn down to make room for MMA waterfront facilities. She sold sewing supplies, clothing, gifts and toys. Ethel and her sister Grace lived in the large house at the corner of Main and Stevens streets. The latter street was known as Murder Alley. Tradition holds that a bloody killing occurred there in the 1800s. The street was avoided by children after dark as it was rumored the ghost of the victim roamed there looking for revenge.

16. Hooper's Garage, a Ford agency, was originally on Sea Street at the north end of the old sardine canning factory where MMA's Andrews Hall is now located. The business was started in 1913 by Merton Hooper, just ten years after Ford Motor Company was established, thus was one of the first dealers in the country of that brand. By the late 1940s the building was in very poor condition, so the owners, Merton and his son Ken built a new place of business on Water Street across from the Ralph Wardwell Insurance office. In 2016, T & C Grocery is the current occupant of that building. Hooper's Garages sold new and used cars, provided automotive service and repair, and sold gasoline.

17. Captain Arthur Ladd operated the *Hippocampus*, a forty-eight foot motor vessel, as a mail, cargo and passenger boat between Castine, Islesboro and Belfast. He made one round trip each weekday from his wharf located south of the Castine town wharf at approximately the current site of MMA's Travelift finger piers. The wharf extended from his storage building and included

a hinged ramp that could be raised or lowered, depending on tide level, to make the end even with the boat's deck. Captain Ladd's business made it possible for travelers in Castine to ride the *Hippocampus* to Belfast, then transfer to the Belfast and Moosehead Railroad train for a ride to a rail junction where the Boston train could be boarded. Thus Castine was connected to the rest of the world by daily public transportation. Captain Ladd also ran special trips for Castine High School students that allowed the girls and boys basketball teams to play the Islesboro High School teams.

18. Noah Hooper was the undertaker in Castine for many years, his place of business being the Acadia Building on the waterfront. The building was sold to Joe and Susan Pederson in the 1950s and became a marina, Acadia Yacht Service. It burned in the 1970s. The location was at the present site of the town's Acadia Wharf. Mr. and Mrs. Hooper lived in the house at 13 Main Street.

19. Dennett Brothers was a waterfront business owned by brothers Jake and Joe Dennett in the building currently occupied by Dennett's Wharf Restaurant and the adjacent residence just to the south. They stored and maintained boats, sold marine supplies, rented boats, provided boat tours in a twenty-five foot motor launch, and sold gasoline for boats and cars. In the winter Jake built rowboats on the second floor of the smaller building. The author remembers Jake as a gruff man who let young boys borrow a rowboat and then would stand at the end of the wharf watching and worrying about their safety. He frequently shouted, "Hey, you kids, si'down in the gawdam boat."

20. Eaton's Boatyard was at the same location it occupies today. This is perhaps the only Castine business that is still in the same family seventy years later. In the 1940s it was a boat-building shop. There was no pier in front of the building, and no marina services were provided, rather Mace Eaton and his son Alonzo

(father of Ken and Larry) built traditional wooden boats, both sail and motor. The designs and workmanship were extraordinary, and there was always a client waiting list. Designs were often from half-models carved by Mace. The author recalls seeing Mace set the waterline of a large power boat that was nearing completion in his shop. He walked the length of the craft pushing common pins through string into the side of the boat at what he gauged to be the waterline. He then applied bottom paint below that line. Somehow he instinctively knew where the boat would float, and when launched, it floated at his predicted waterline. The launching of a new boat was a festive affair with many town residents and visitors attending.

21. Castine Coal Company, selling coal and propane gas, had facilities on the shore northeast of Eaton's Boatyard. Originally a wharf extended from the shore, and coal was brought by boat or barge. That wharf collapsed prior to about 1945, depositing a large amount of coal on the beach, pieces of which may still be found there. After the loss of the wharf, coal was brought to Bucksport by rail, then to Castine by truck. A building (no longer there) on Water Street was used as one storage facility and a second was in the basement of the house opposite Hooper's Garage on Water Street. The company was originally owned by the Wheeler family who lived in the house at the north corner of Perkins and Pleasant streets. In 1950 the business was purchased by the author's parents, Harrison and Helen Small. She did all of the office work, he did propane installations, and Lawrence (Lossie) Littlefield drove the truck delivering coal and propane tanks. When the Smalls bought the business they increased Lossie's salary by 25 percent, bringing it up to twenty-five dollars per week. On slow days in the summer, Lossie would occasionally take the author out in a rowboat, tying up at the bell buoy to fish. We stopped along the way to

dig clams for bait plus enough for him to eat fresh from the shell. On our most successful trip we returned with a thirty-five pound cod. Or maybe it was thirty-two pounds.

22. Castine Hospital was located on Court Street in the building currently housing the Castine Community Health Service. Dr. Harold Babcock was the physician; his wife Till, a nurse, did anesthesiology. Other nurses included Beulah Rowell, Vernice Rowell and Therma Douglas. Surgery was performed, bones were set, babies were delivered, and assorted ills taken care of. Dr. Robert Russell joined the hospital staff shortly after 1950. Patients came from many towns in the area, including Castine, Penobscot, Orland, Brooksville, Bucksport, Deer Isle and Stonington.

23. Alva Clement, carpenter, had a shop in one of the buildings next to his house at 120 Court Street. Around 1950 he built a new shop across the street which, sixty-six years later, still bears a faded sign proclaiming "A.D. CLEMENT, CARPENTER." Alva's business was mainly concerned with building and repairing houses. His employees included Emory Witham, Woodrow Bakeman and Claire Williams, all Castine residents. His wife, Lorna Douglas Clement, was active in a number of organizations in town and was written about in the 1942 best-selling book *The Little Locksmith.*

24. Walter Farley was a carpenter who worked mainly by himself and on smaller projects than Alva did. He and his wife lived at 124 Water Street, and the house to the left of that property was his shop.

25. Marie Wardwell Wood sold dairy farm supplies, including milk bottle caps, to farmers in the area, and she had a taxi license. She became the first woman to be elected as a town selectman, and was a member of the Maine State Legislature. She lived in a house at 112 Water Street that was moved "off the neck" near One-mile Corner in 1997.

26. Joel Perkins was a house painter and lived at 111 Water Street. He usually worked by himself or with his son.

27. Roy Bowden did carpentry, electrical and masonry work. He and his wife Alice lived at a number of locations both in town and off the neck, their final residence being the house at 136 Perkins Street, which Roy built.

28. Owen Porter was a master electrician who did residential electrical installation and repair. He and his wife lived on Battle Avenue in "Birch Lodge" near the lighthouse.

29. Henry Devereux installed and repaired plumbing and heating systems. He and his wife Charlene lived on Court Street in the house directly across from Emerson Hall. Charlene was active in local community and high school theater productions.

30. Verne Hooper also did plumbing and heating work. He was originally from Campobello Island, New Brunswick, and came to Castine to work in the sardine factory. After it closed, he apprenticed to Henry Devereux and about 1950 started his own business, which continued for twenty years. At one time Verne owned a Pierce Arrow coupe automobile that was much admired by young boys.

31. Donald Hutchins ran a house-painting business with his shop in the garage next to the swimming pool and across the street from his house near the back shore. He employed several people in this business.

32. Leonard (Link) Sawyer owned the third house-painting business in Castine. He and his wife Geneva lived in the house they had built at 35 Tarratine Street. Link was assisted by Leander (Stubb) Perkins who lived with his wife Susan near the top of Pleasant Street. Susan worked at the post office.

33. Geneva Sawyer (Link's wife) was a cook who ran a catering business and also prepared the golf club suppers every Thursday and Sunday during July and August.

A sketch of downtown Castine by Jay Pratt.

34. May Wardwell operated a beauty shop in her home at 10 Perkins Street. Her husband Carl is mentioned above as having a grocery store on Main Street.

35. Roger Danforth raised vegetables and laying hens at his farm on the Shore Road. In addition, he had a blueberry field in town at the present site of Hatch's Cove subdivision. Roger also was a land surveyor. Ethelyn Danforth taught at Adams School. They lived at 103 Court Street.

36. Mervin Wood, with the help of his family, raised broiler chickens at their farm on the Shore Road near Roger Danforth's farm. In the early 1950s he purchased two other properties for raising chickens, both on the Castine Road, one in Castine and the other in Penobscot. One of his sons is the retired owner of Gary's Fuel Service.

37. Phillip Babcock, son of Dr. Babcock, was the proprietor of "Weary Acres Farm" on the Shore Road where he raised laying hens. His wife, Margery Leach Babcock, was a teacher at Adams School for many years.

38. Francis (Cooler) Sawyer operated a farm on the Castine Road and raised dairy cows and pigs. The property is still owned by family members.

39. Laurelie Farm, located at the end of Mill Lane and facing the back shore, was owned by George McGuire. Beef cattle were raised there. Keith Apt was employed as the farmer, and his family lived in a house on the farm. The property is still owned by relatives of Mr. McGuire.

40. Fernwood Farm, on the Castine Road, was run by the Hamm family for several years in the early 1950s as a dairy farm. Later, the property was purchased by Mervin Wood to raise broiler chickens. The farmhouse, a very old Cape dating perhaps from the 1700s, was torn down in the 1970s.

41. Noah Hooper, the undertaker, had a fox farm that was originally located near Mayo Point but later moved to a site which is now the mobile home park on the Shore Road. Foxes and minks were raised for their pelts, and the farm was operated by Charles Colson, whose son Donald became a television newscaster in Bangor and in Texas. Donald's son Craig has followed his father in career choice.

42. William Dunbar was a land surveyor and part-time farmer. He and wife, Lowena, lived on the Castine Road.

43. Gunroom Booksellers, a store dealing in old books, was run by Alan and Mary Wescott from their home on the Castine Road. The house had been in the Wescott family since it was built around 1800. Mr. Wescott's early life was considerable more exciting than that of most booksellers. As a very young teenager he ran away from home to join a circus. At the start of World War I he enlisted in the Royal Canadian Army at about fifteen years of age and served in Europe.

44. Nina Macomber taught several generations of reluctant young pianists from her home, the house at 11 Tarratine Street, where she lived with her husband,Harry.

45. Victor Black owned a thirty-foot fishing boat that he used for lobstering during warmer months of the year and scalloping during the winter. The author remembers being sent by his mother to Dennett's Wharf on winter afternoons carrying a pint jar and a dollar bill. Victor would fill the jar with the newly shucked scallops in exchange for the dollar.

46. Frederick Guild owned and captained several coastal schooners that carried summer vacationers on week-long cruises in Penobscot Bay. The boats were among the first of the Maine windjammer fleet. One of them, *Victory Chimes*, a three-masted schooner, is still carrying summer passengers. In winter, Capt. Guild, assisted by Stub Perkins, fished for scallops. Both businesses were run from the Guild home, the handsome 1800 house on Route 166 that overlooks Hatch's Cove. Janet Guild's recipe for "Scallops à la Castine" is still used by some Castine residents.

47. The Castine Inn was, as now, one of several summer hotels. It was owned by Nell Mercer who also owned the Brunswick Hotel on Copley Square in Boston.

48. The Holiday House, another summer hotel, was the building that is now a summer residence at 147 Perkins Street. It was owned by Rodney (Buffy) Gray, then sold to the Allen family in the early 1950s.

49. The Pentagöet Inn, with a series of owners including Mr. and Mrs. Adam Beaumont, was operated on a year-round basis. Mr. Beaumont was a retired diplomat.

50. The Manor, originally a summer cottage, was operated as a seasonal hotel and then closed for several years. Joseph and

Susan Pederson purchased and reopened it as a summer hotel in the 1950s.

51. The Blake House was a bed-and-breakfast, although that term may not have been part of our language in 1950. It was owned by Mrs. Blake and her daughter Seritta, who had a black Buick convertible and a black Newfoundland dog who greeted guests. It was in the 1800 house on the east corner of Main and Court streets.

52. A tiny grocery store, located on Court Street across from the MMA football field, was run by several siblings of the McKinnon family, who lived in the house next door. The building, no longer there, was only about fifteen feet square, and thus had a limited selection of products. MMA baseball and football games brought many customers looking for snack foods and soda.

53. Gene Bowden had a food take-out stand at the town wharf parking area. It was in a trailer that he towed to the site in spring and removed after the summer season was over. He served hotdogs, hamburgers, lobster rolls, fries and soft drinks. The parking area was not paved at that time, and the gravel surface was the location of horseshoe games most evenings in the summer. Gene was one of the major players. Car owners learned that it was not a good idea to park vehicles near the horseshoe pits, as errant shoes sometimes tumbled out of control with players taunting the thrower, "You forgot to take the shoe off the horse."

54. Wilburt (Winky) Gray trapped foxes, raccoons, and bobcats for the fur market. He lived in what was originally the Methodist parsonage at 81 Court Street.

55. Merton (Spunk) Hatch was a trapper, drove the school bus and raised strawberries. He provided jobs to teenaged girls picking berries. He would not hire boys as they ate too many berries, and they started fights throwing the strawberries at each

other. Merton, Laura and their four sons lived at the top of Tarratine Street.

56. Maine Maritime Academy was much smaller than now with about two hundred students. It was established in 1941 and took over the buildings that had previously been the Eastern State Normal School. MMA's program was just eighteen months long during World War II, then expanded to three years after the war. It was a year-round program with two majors, deck or engine. Graduates earned Bachelor of Science degrees. There were three buildings at the top of Pleasant Street: Dismukes Hall with classrooms; Leavitt Hall, the dormitory and cafeteria; and Quick Hall, the gymnasium. All students lived in the dormitory. The football/baseball field was at the current location, at the corner of Court and Pleasant streets. The waterfront campus included several old buildings housing a machine shop and a welding shop plus the wharf with training ship, *American Sailor*. Nearly all MMA employees lived in Castine, some in Academy-owned housing, but many owned their homes.

57. The MMA Book and Clothing Store was primarily for students, but anyone could shop the inventory of books and uniform clothes. It was located in the east corner of Dismukes Hall basement, and was run by Lloyd Farley, Walter Farley's brother.

58. Charles Parker, Bert's son, opened a shop in Willis Ricker's building on Water Street around 1946. He sold cameras and film in addition to plying his trade as a photographer. The business lasted only a short time. Mrs. Parker, Leah, taught at Adams School, and I understand that their son, Tim, became a popular Maine comedian.

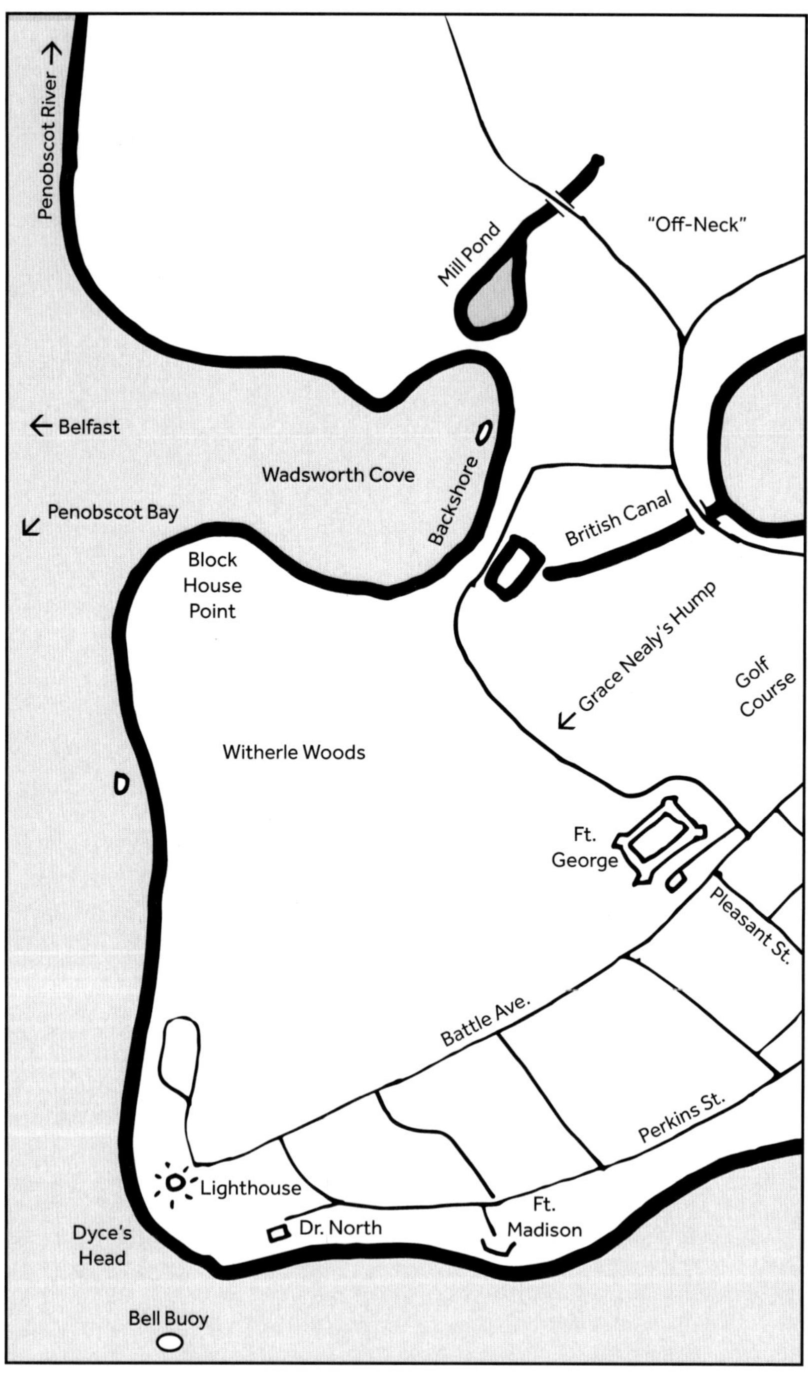
Penobscot River
"Off-Neck"
Mill Pond
Belfast
Wadsworth Cove
Backshore
Penobscot Bay
British Canal
Block
House
Point
Grace Nealy's Hump
Golf
Course
Witherle Woods
Ft.
George
Pleasant St.
Battle Ave.
Perkins St.
Lighthouse
Ft.
Madison
Dr. North
Dyce's
Head
Bell Buoy

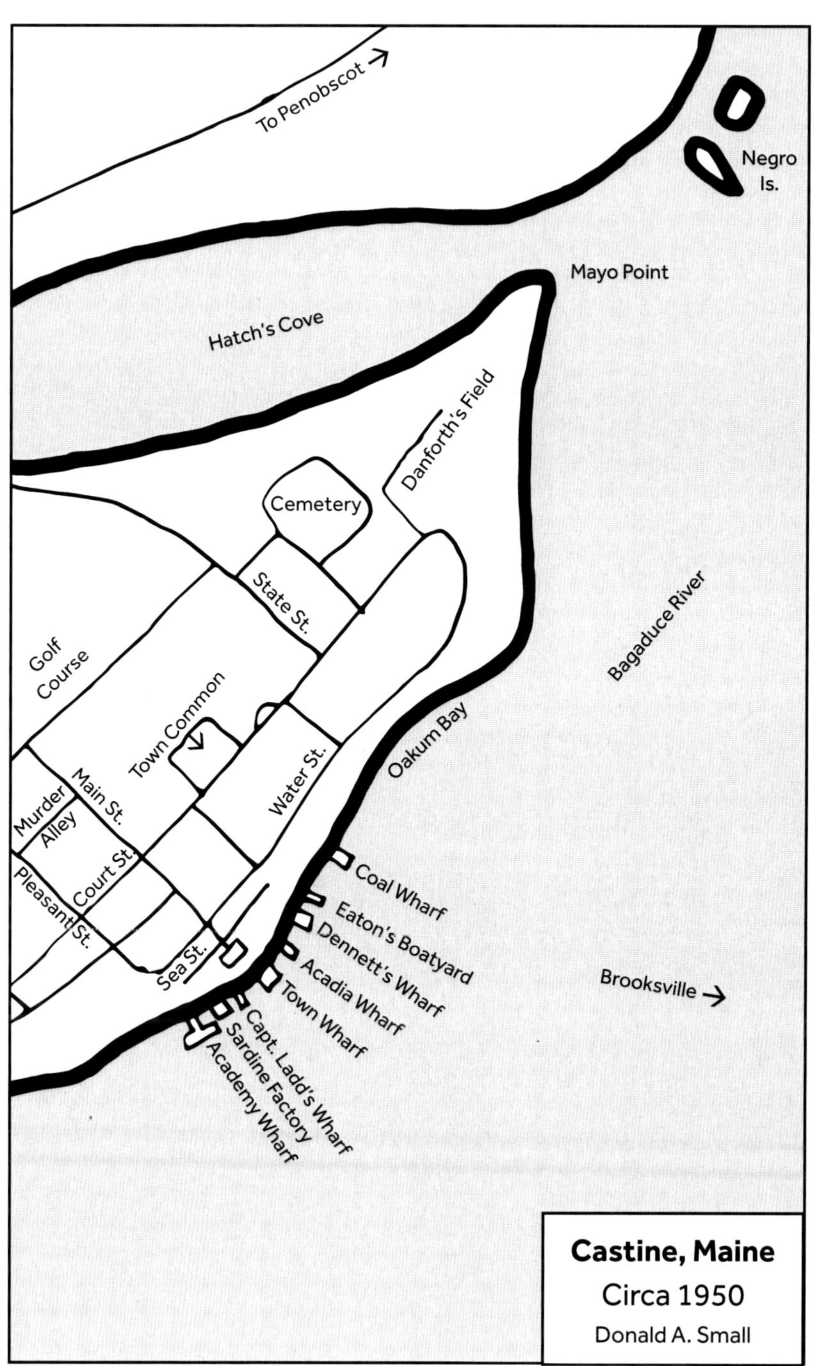
To Penobscot
Negro Is.
Mayo Point
Hatch's Cove
Danforth's Field
Cemetery
State St.
Bagaduce River
Golf Course
Town Common
Oakum Bay
Water St.
Main St.
Murder Alley
Court St.
Pleasant St.
Sea St.
Coal Wharf
Eaton's Boatyard
Dennett's Wharf
Acadia Wharf
Town Wharf
Capt. Ladd's Wharf
Sardine Factory
Academy Wharf
Brooksville
Castine, Maine
Circa 1950
Donald A. Small

About the author

Donald Small spent his childhood in Castine where he attended the local grammar school and filled his summers with excursions into Witherle Woods, swimming at the Back Shore and salt water pool, caddying and learning to play golf, riding his bicycle, mowing neighbors' lawns, and camping on islands in the Bagaduce River. It was a time when children over the age of about six years were allowed, even expected, to fend for themselves on any day they were not in school. Apparently the modern term for allowing this heady freedom is "free-ranging" and is frowned on by some, but in 1950 it was the norm.

Small attended Castine High School, graduating in 1956, one of five in that year's class. The small number of students in the school meant that all had to participate in most activities. There were boys basketball and baseball teams, so he played those sports (not very well, though). He sang in the school chorus, performed in theater productions, and participated in student council. His English teacher encouraged him to write, and he won a state essay contest, but did not continue with a writing career.

He attended the University of Maine and spent six years attempting to learn something of engineering. Following graduate school he worked in industry doing research and developing new equipment. He lived in several locations around the United States and Canada, but eventually returned to Castine where he enjoyed teaching engineering courses at Maine Maritime Academy for thirty years before retirement.

Small lives in Castine with his wife, Shelley, also a retired teacher. Two daughters and their families, including grandchildren, live in nearby towns. He volunteers with several local organizations. Other activities, in addition to writing, include woodworking, music, travel, boating, walking, golf, and entertaining the family dog.

A selection of other titles available from

Penobscot Books

A division of Penobscot Bay Press

Around Maine — A coloring book for all who love the Pine Tree State
by Jean Lamontanaro $11.95

How to Catch a Lobster — Spend a day with Ed and Anne Black as they fish for lobster. For children and their adults
by Leslie Moore $16.95

Sage Advice from Uncle Oscar — Boyhood memories of Blue Hill
by Sage Collins $22.95

Island Naturalist — 2015 Maine Literary Awards Winner
by Kathie Fiveash $27.95

Floating Palaces — America's Queens of the Sea
Maine Island Mariners and the Big Steam Yachts
by William A. Haviland and Barbara L. Britton $33.95

GOTCHA! April Fool! — Humorous spoofs published in Penobscot Bay Press newspapers 1964-2012
by Jerry Durnbaugh and others $25.95

An Island Sense of Home: Stories from Isle au Haut
by Harold S. van Doren $37.95

I Loved This Work....I have been delightfully busy
by John T. Crowell with accompanying DVD $49.95

Centennial: A Century of Island Newspapers
by James M. Aldrich $24.95

P.O. Box 36, 69 Main St. Stonington ME 04681
books@pbp.me • *penbaypress.me*
207-367-2200